# This Earth, My Brother . . .

Kofi Awoonor

HEINEMANN
London · Ibadan · Nairobi

Heinemann Educational Books
48 Charles Street London W1X 8AH
P.M.B. 5205 Ibadan · P.O. BOX 25080 Nairobi
EDINBURGH MELBOURNE TORONTO AUCKLAND
NEW DELHI SINGAPORE HONG KONG KUALA LUMPUR
ISBN 0 435 90108 7 (paperback)

First published in *African Writers Series* 1972

Printed in Great Britain by Cox & Wyman Ltd,
London, Reading and Fakenham

AFRICAN WRITERS SERIES

**108 · Kofi Awoonor · *This Earth, My Brother . . .***

1 Chinua Achebe: *Things Fall Apart*
2 Cyprian Ekwensi: *Burning Grass*
3 Chinua Achebe: *No Longer at Ease*
4 Kenneth Kaunda: *Zambia Shall be Free*
5 Cyprian Ekwensi: *People of the City*
6 Peter Abrahams: *Mine Boy*
7 James Ngugi: *Weep Not Child*
8 John Reed and Clive Wake (Editors): *A Book of African Verse*
9 Richard Rive: *Modern African Prose*
10 Paul Edwards (Editor): *Equiano's Travels*
11 T. M. Aluko: *One Man, One Matchet*
12 William Conton: *The African*
13 Mongo Beti: *Mission to Kala*
14 Richard Rive, Alex La Guma, James Matthews and Alf Wannenburgh: *Quartet*
15 David Cook (Editor): *Origin East Africa*
16 Chinua Achebe: *Arrow of God*
17 James Ngugi: *The River Between*
18 Obotunde Ijimere: *The Imprisonment of Obatala and other plays*
19 Cyprian Ekwensi: *Lokotown and other stories*
20 Mugo Gatheru: *Child of Two Worlds*
21 John Munonye: *The Only Son*
22 Lenrie Peters: *The Second Round*
23 Ulli Beier (Editor): *The Origin of Life and Death*
24 Aubrey Kachingwe: *No Easy Task*
25 Elechi Amadi: *The Concubine*
26 Flora Nwapa: *Efuru*
27 Francis Selormey: *The Narrow Path*
28 David Cook and Miles Lee (Editors): *Short East African Plays*
29 Ferdinand Oyono: *Houseboy*
30 T. M. Aluko: *One Man, One Wife*
31 Chinua Achebe: *A Man of the People*
32 T. M. Aluko: *Kinsman and Foreman*
33 Stanlake Samkange: *On Trial for my Country*
34 Cosmo Pieterse (Editor): *Ten One-Act Plays*
35 Alex La Guma: *A Walk in the Night a*[illegible] *other stories*
36 James Ngugi: *A Grain of Wheat*
37 Lenrie Peters: *Satellites*
38 Oginga Odinga: *Not yet Uhuru*
39 Ferdinand Oyono: *The Old Man and* [illegible] *Medal*
40 S. A. Konadu: *A Woman in Her Prime*
41 Amu Djoleto: *The Strange Man*
42 Kofi Awoonor and G. Adali-Mortty (Editors): *Messages–Poems from Ghana*
43 Ayi Kwei Armah: *The Beautyful Ones Are Not Yet Born*
44 Elechi Amadi: *The Great Ponds*
45 John Munonye: *Obi*
46 Dennis Brutus: *Letters to Martha and other poems*
47 Tayeb Salih: *The Wedding of Zein*
48 Bakare Gbadamosi and Ulli Beier: *Not Even God is Ripe Enough*
49 Kwame Nkrumah: *Neo-Colonialism*
50 J. P. Clark: *America, their America*
51 James Ngugi: *The Black Hermit*
52 Sahle Sellassie: *The Afersata*
53 Peter K. Palangyo: *Dying in the Sun*
54 Robert Serumaga: *Return to the Shadows*
55 S. A. Konadu: *Ordained by the Oracle*
56 Flora Nwapa: *Idu*
57 Mbella Sonne Dipoko: *Because of Women*
58 Ulli Beier (Editor): *Political Spider and other stories*
59 Bediako Asare: *Rebel*
60 Luis Bernardo Honwana: *We Killed Mangy Dog and other stories*
61 Rems Nna Umeasiegbu: *The Way We Lived*
62 Christopher Okigbo: *Labyrinths*
63 Sembene Ousmane: *God's Bits of Wood*
64 Cosmo Pieterse (Editor): *Seven South African Poets*
65 Duro Ladipo: *Three Plays*
66 Tayeb Salih: *Season of Migration to the North*
67 Nkem Nwankwo: *Danda*
68 Gabriel Okara: *The Voice*
69 Taban lo Liyong: *Fixions*
70 T. M. Aluko: *Chief The Honourable Minister*
71 L. S. Senghor: *Nocturnes*
72 Tchicaya U Tam'si: *Selected Poems*
73 Len Ortzen: *North African Writing*
74 Taban lo Liyong: *Eating Chiefs*
75 Jan Knappert: *Myths and Legends of the Swahili*
76 Wole Soyinka: *The Interpreters*
[illegible] *rus*
[illegible] r): *Short African* [illegible]
[illegible] *rs to the Past*
[illegible]: *From a Crooked Rib*
[illegible] a: *The Challenge of Nation-* [illegible]
[illegible] Sonne Dipoko: *A Few Nights and Days*
83 Jan Knappert: *Myths and Legends of the Congo*
84 Cyprian Ekwensi: *Beautiful Feathers*
85 Onuora Nzekwu: *Wand of Noble Wood*
86 Francis Bebey: *Agatha Moudio's Son*
87 Bernard B. Dadié: *Climbié*
88 Mongo Beti: *The Poor Christ of Bomba*

89 Pat Amadu Maddy: *Obasai and Other Plays*
90 Taban lo Liyong: *Frantz Fanon's Uneven Ribs*
91 Onuora Nzekwu: *Blade Among the Boys*
92 Sembene Ousmane: *The Money Order & White Genesis*
93 Jan Knappert: *A Choice of Flowers*
94 John Munonye: *Oil Man of Obange*
95 Sonallah Ibrahim: *The Smell of It*
96 David Cook and David Rubadiri (Editors): *Poems from East Africa*
97 Ali A. Mazrui: *The Trial of Christopher Okigbo*
98 Dominic Mulaisho: *The Tongue of the Dumb*
99 Yambo Ouologuem: *Bound to Violence*
100 Chinua Achebe: *Girls at War and other stories*
101 Bessie Head: *Maru*
102 Kole Omotoso: *The Edifice*
103 Lenrie Peters: *Katchikali*
104 Can Themba: *The Will to Die*
105 Bonnie Lubega: *The Outcasts*
106 John Reed and Clive Wake (Editors): *French African Verse*
107 Mbella Sonne Dipoko: *Black & White in Love*
108 Kofi Awoonor: *This Earth, My Brother ...*

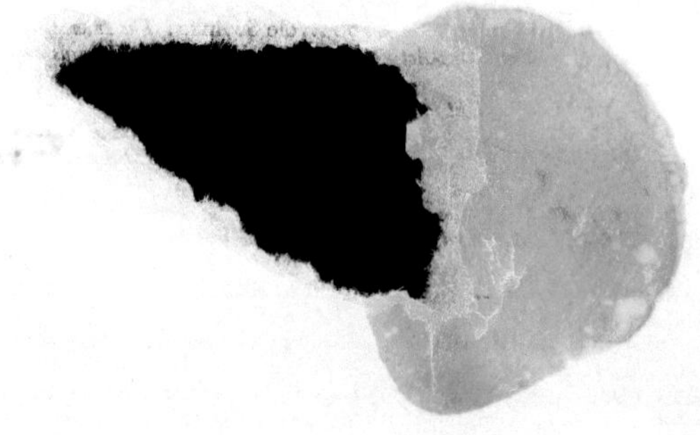

To my children, Sika, Dunyo and Kalepe, that they will grow and understand these words.

This is an allegory in which all the names of the characters are entirely fictitious.

In the middle of the journey of our life I came to myself within a dark wood where the straight way was lost. Ah, how hard a thing it is to tell of that wood, savage and harsh and dense, the thought of which renews my fear! So bitter is it that death is hardly more.

DANTE'S INFERNO. CANTO I

# This Earth, My Brother . . .

So they said, this is it. I know them all. They are pretending not to be looking at me; casting furtive glances, and withdrawing their eyes like hawks that give not to their offspring, averting their eyes. As if I wanted something off their backs. They knew. I didn't ask them for anything. When I say it, then they become gentle and they pretend. Show him sympathy. He is a well-educated man, they say. He comes from a great family. He went to England, read books, big fat books of wisdom. I planted the tree of wisdom. I hoed the field of thorns, collected and burned the thistles on the outskirts, and planted the tree. Yes. When I went to see her, she pretended not to recognize my knock on the door. My knock! She used to jump up. She read my steps from afar. She said she smelled me from far away.

Was it a busy day?

Yes.

Silence. Silence.

She would wear her pink nightie, underneath it the violence of her nipples black thick and cruel. Then she would laugh. Because I touched her in the armpit. Yes, touched her. It wasn't funny. She would laugh, a shrill little laugh revealing the gap where a tooth was extracted while I waited outside the dentist's office.

Was it a busy day?

No.

Silence.

No?

No.

But you look tired. Take off your shoes. Sit down. Then she would sit down first, carelessly, revealing her ass. She would wear a blue skirt and a scarlet blouse.

Are you hungry?

No.

No?

No.

Silence.

When I planted the tree after hoeing the field of thorns, I burned the harvest of thistles. I went to the public tap and washed my hands and drank some water. Then she revealed her ass, the hair on it was black, thick combed upwards. She sat down holding and caressing her left thigh. Her eyes vacant. Staring.

Are you sure?

About what?

I am not sure about anything. I am not. How many times must I tell her that I am not sure!

She said she smelled me. She read my steps at all hours. In her sleep she knew it when I walked towards her room. Even if I didn't knock, she would open the door. The other night I came, she said, her river was in flood. So I couldn't ride in my canoe. I said I would. She said, It is a taboo. Taboo my ass. When she showed fright I said I would go away. She said, No, don't go away. Stay with me. I am frightened. Of what? Of me of course. She thought I would do her some physical injury; twist her arms and legs or slap her face, and kill her in a fit of anger as in one of those deeds of passion.

She would walk towards her little bed. I bought it for her. And the mattress. She would lie down and say, Let me take off your shoes. Come and lie down awhile. You look tired. She would take off my shoes slowly. And I would go towards the bed, lie by her side. I would squeeze her hand gently as she caressed me. Gently. I would take her, hard and gentle, and she would complain of bruises in her woman. And I would say it was not my fault. After her eyes had turned into white, the brown pupils gone, and she had gasped, and cried and scratched, she would quieten down. And sigh. Then I would hold her throat with my big hand. And squeeze it hard and gentle. She would moan and cry and not move. Slowly her eyes would run, the brown vanishing far away to the world's end where graves are green and white with stones. Slowly, very slowly, I would let her die.

I came back the next noon, through the rain, mud on my brown shoes, stepping into puddles, into gutters of nights and days raining hard here in this land. The gentle drizzle I am not aware of forming a filmy halo of mist rising from my head heat of headache which no pills could cure. She would lie there breathing gently in a soft liquid sleep and wake up and look at me with those sad eyes misty with little tears. Like the one that freshened a long-ago cactus in a deserted garden far away, of my friend and brother Jesus. Then I would be sorry I had killed her. And I would go on my knees and beg her that I would never kill her again so long as I lived; that I would die in her place should they want to kill her, beat her and shame her in this land of ours. I would take all the indignities and the shames intended for her, I would cry hard like a man, and say, It is the death of a woman which is far away. Man's is near, hiding behind his door.

Then I would rise from the floor on my knees marked by the patterns on the linoleum, and slowly I would return from where I came.

A mermaid was sitting on my lap. Dripping water. Her feet, tail were fins spread-eagled in fans. Sitting on my lap. Her eyes were rolling in circles of little fires, her breasts balls of flames; she was breathing pollen gold and cinnamon down my neck; her teeth rows of sapphires and corals. She was shedding tears of moondust.

> My strength is dried up like a potsherd; and my
> tongue cleaveth to my jaws; and thou hast
> brought me into the dust of death.

I would renew my oath, my promise that I would never kill her again; that it was my error. No, I shall let her live within me. Let her share my joy. My agony I shall keep away from her in the firm belief that she will never die.

> Deliver my soul from the sword; my darling
> from the power of the dog.

I shall ask her deliverance from the terror and the burden of this joy. Her corals and sapphires shall be planted upon my neck, incisors stamping marks I shall wear in little crosses of the thunder initiates till my dying day.

Then she was no longer a mermaid. She became the overseer in our ward. A squat ugly man with the voice of a dog barking in my sleep every night. He was marching up and down with a long bamboo cane. He stamped his feet in military precision just to impress and frighten us. Pretending he didn't know we were there.

She was her, my mermaid sitting on my lap, dripping wet with water now crying now laughing. I stretched forth my hand to squeeze her breasts. They felt like flames, black blue flames of the burning of the spirit, bursting in my hand in gold.

She was my mermaid come from the sea. She came one night when the moon was there, burning over the ocean. Her beams cast upon the spire of our wooden church built by the missionaries from Bremen in 1847. They died. They are all buried in the churchyard beside the chapel with shiny words in German on the gravestones made of marble.

That moon that night was singing in the season of mackerel when fishermen cast their nets in the night to prepare to haul in a good catch at dawn just when the women were leaving morning service. Mackerels screaming the gulls gone home to bird island and we lay in the sand waiting.

Then she came up. Head first. Upon the water at the spot where the steamers used to stop in those days, on the line of the biggest moonray she emerged. Head first. Her hair was long and black and shining like flames of jet streaming down her long thin body which has now become flabby with age and time and labour. Then she rose from the sea, casting about her a flaming mantle of beaten cloth, her breasts shiny and erect upon the water. I could not see any more.

She walked the sandy lanes of my home town with me. We skirted the shoreline that night and many more nights. She was my secret; no one else saw her by my side. They could not see her. The second day my father said, You look like a sleepwalker. You have neglected your daily chores; you no longer read your Reader Six. You disobey your elders.

She was with me. And I was not afraid. I told her my story of the nature and the bitterness of the birthwater that nurtured me. Of the womb that carried me. Of the pangs that delivered me. She listened. She never said a word. Only she would smile a knowing smile, revealing her teeth of coral and sapphires. We walked the edges of the big lagoon. I pointed out to her where the gulls return at night on bird island. We followed the tracks laid by infant fisher feet of the tegayi where a shiny shoal of fish in the mud and the long line of retrievers followed bringing home the harvest of fish of the following feet.

When I asked her, Are you tired? she shook her head and her

long hair dropped millions of golden stars behind her. If I stopped to collect them she would rebuke me. Then we would walk on, through marsh. We would walk on. She wanted to know who owned what portion. What happened to the owners of this neglected compound? Who owned this house whose fences were falling and termites ate the shiny trees that held it together?

The third night I said I was tired. We had wandered again the whole night. We sat underneath the Indian almond tree on the beach, just about two hundred and ten yards from the spot where she came out that night long ago I cannot remember how recently. My feet were tired from the long walks, my head ached violently from lack of rest. The boys and girls from our households had been looking for me for days. That night my mother had joined them, a hurricane lantern swinging in her hand as she led the chorus of querulous and talkative children to look for me. Always they would pass me by without seeing me. Sometimes as near as one yard, or sometimes one foot. They swept past like a band of choristers calling my names and looking behind every tin shack, and behind every tree. They came so close that day I could hear their talk.

Where could he have gone?

He hasn't come home to eat his food!

They said, He didn't show up at the school.

She stood close to me breathing down my neck cinnamon.

The moon had arisen that night again, like the night she came. She shone in a violent fire of long line like the glinting knife. Carving the sea in two where that night she came. It was blazing in the silence of the long knife to the foot of the Indian almond; it blazed. She stood near me, her eyes reflecting the blaze of the fiery water in the savagery of the carving knife. Then it began to happen.

First the whale, the rolling stone tree trunk deity, is the worshipper of thunder, dalosu, the seer and the unseen, the rider of the white horse of the air in the sky above his children. He rolled up in his majesty without hindrance. Then he rested in the sand at the edge of the silver foam where they covet gold out of old coffins of dead buried on land now covered by the waters of the sea long ago, my father said when he was a boy.

From the sea the worshippers emerged. They were led by a tall man clad in white. Around his head a blue band in which flamed the tail feather of a parrot. He held the long spear rattler and a small group of gong boys followed him beating time to the fall of his rattler that shook with its bells. Then there came an host of women, bare-chested, their drooping breasts flapping about their chests, their skins shining with shea butter in the violet light of the single moonbeam that slashed the sea in two. They were not singing. From their lips rose an ululation long, echoing among the fallen walls behind the church bell. Then they would slap their hands over their mouths interrupting for split seconds the long cry. They were looking for the dead, in every corner, in every tin shack, in every fallen-down mud house. Behind them came a long line of teenagers. Boys. Long-limbed boys with small feet flat in the sand. Girls. Their breasts scarcely out bubbling. Their bodies shining in shea butter. Each had around her waist long agrey beads of several colours. Their rears singed in white chalk, studded with ground black incense of the sycamore. They were not singing. Their heads bent upon the earth, as their feet traced many footsteps in the sand following the tall man with the rattler.

At the end of the line, around the body of the whale a circle formed. The ululation stopped. The leader lifted his hand up into the skies. The followers bent their heads upon the earth.

Then they sang a song. A low moan, mournful song of death, and loss. The moon blazed on. She sent a sword that divided the sea and cast itself upon the black shiny body of the whale.

After what seemed like a day, the ululation died down. The line was led again by the tall man. The boys and the girls followed. Then the whale in his majesty. She, as in a dream, moved from my side under the Indian almond. Into the burning sword of the moonbeam which carved at the sea they all moved to the single jangle of the leader's rattler. She was the last to go.

And I was alone. But not for long.

## ••• Chapter 1

Deme lies on the great northern road that cuts across the abdomen of Eweland heading towards Kete Krachi, towards the north. It lies thirty miles to the sea, from the market-town of Keta. Its people are a wing of the Anlo sojourners from Notsie several years ago. Not even the very old can remember how long ago.

The lorry road is a narrow track of red earth beaten together by many feet, and the few trucks that careered along it on market-days on their way to the coast. It was mainly built, if it was built at all, of mud, and gravel collected by women from the gravel pits beneath the Aka River. When it rained, it was closed to traffic. There was a road overseer, a fat, drunken man who could be seen after the second day of rain in his army supply raincoat, carrying a large load of keys which he jingled with a great deal of the feeling of importance. Then he would move to the northern end of the town and close the creaking gate under the tall Ago palm, and return to his house in the sweaty expectation that the drivers of the plantain and yam trucks would come around and offer him gifts. He had been at his post for years, no one knew how long. He and the creaking gate under the Ago palm were indistinguishable. The gate was the symbol of his authority. The epiphany of his power as an agent of the government at Accra.

The lorries would form a long line on both sides of this gate. The drivers who didn't have any gifts to give lurched out into the market-square and sought out the palm wine stalls while their passengers sat on the wooden planks and dozed for days. The few that could offer a gift sauntered in and out of the road overseer's house, and split with him never-ending bottles of akpeteshie, the home-made gin declared illegal by the colonial government. He himself sat in his easy chair in his parlour, a veritable picture of human lethargy translated into power at its most resigned and unconcerned pivot.

The only time that he came to life was when one of his many

assistants ran up and reported the arrival of a touring car. A car signified a white man and the lowliest minion of the Empire must be about his duty. England expects every man to do his duty. Then Mr Attipoe would jump off his chair, his bulk and his state of drunkenness notwithstanding. His small red eyes would come to life. And, like a sleepwalker, he would dash off pursued by a group of excited drivers who fondly hoped their chance had come to continue their journeys. If it was a false alarm, Mr Attipoe would return cursing his assistants. The dogs, didn't they know he was resting? Anyone who reported false fire next time would lose his job. Then it wasn't he, Attipoe Esquire, road overseer, Deme, who held power over who came and went on the King's road.

Most things came to a standstill when the rains came in Deme. For the rains would come down in great, white sheets beating a dissonant music on the few zinc roofings for days and nights. The intervals that arose were only changed quickly by flashes of thunder and the firing of heavenly muskets. Then the noise and the fury of the rain would rise loud and crashing for hours. Everyone would be indoors. If your house leaked, you gathered together pans and pots in which the drip, drip, drip of the rain beat at first singular tattoos, and then changed to the drop, drop, drop of collecting water. A fire would be lit. The children would gather round it and watch the blaze while their elders warmed their insides with local gin.

Then the rains would clear, and the sun would come out on an early morning. The earth would still be soggy and mud tracks would lead from hut to hut, from house to house, laid by the feet of those who went to drink. Children who had played in the early rains would still be sleeping in the fond hope that it would continue to rain for ever.

The sun had just risen after such a rain over Deme. Kodzo Dzide, the town crier, had spent the night on Mr Attipoe's compound. There had been a wake the previous night. Since that was his seventh wake in the last two days, he had passed out comfortably in a corner near the chicken coop. He opened his eyes, rubbed his face with his palm and looked around to make sure where he was. Women were bustling around bathing children or preparing the morning fires with which to boil water.

His head was sick. Very sick. He remembered just faintly the previous wake at Yenaye. How he came to be at Deme he couldn't remember. His head was sick, he was sure, because he hadn't eaten the previous night.

His wife had left him three markets ago. But man must bear all his troubles. Kodzo was not prepared to go after his wife in spite of the linguist stick sent to him by the chief of his wife's village. He should have heeded his late uncle's advice. He should not have married the woman. The woman had lived in the mining town of Akwatia up country. Any woman who had lived in Akwatia was a prostitute. His uncle said so. Kodzo agreed, nodded his head, as he sat on a log of wood in Mr Attipoe's compound. He was agreeing in memory. He was responsible for his own doom. A goat who visits somebody's house should not weep because its head has been cracked with a club.

His headache returned, sharp jabs of pain caught him on the forehead. He bent his head down and spat the night spittle still in his mouth, bitter and unpleasant. A little naked boy stood in front of him scratching his left foot with his raised right foot, sucking his fingers.

What is your name?

Adonu.

Why haven't you had your prick cut?

No. My father said they will cut it for me when I grow up.

Who is your father?

Road overseer.

Eh, are you road overseer's son?

Yes.

Which woman's son are you?

My mother is from Kuli.

Kosiwo?

Yes.

Then I am your uncle. You hear?

Yes.

Go and fetch me water to wash my face.

During this short exchange, Kodzo heard his stomach rumble like the trumpeting of elephants. And he knew that his hernia was up in arms. After he washed his face, he gathered his cloth and made towards the wooden gates held together by Ago beams towards his own house.

On the way home, he remembered that Mr Attipoe had asked him to beat the gong that morning. He had asked him over four days ago. He even gave him his drink money of a shilling. But what message he was to announce to the town he had forgotten.

He hurried onwards in his jerky walk in which his heels did not touch the ground. This was the result of the long attack of yaws he suffered as a boy.

He pushed his door and stepped inside his damp mud and thatched hut in Ablome, the eastern division of Deme. There was no water in the duck's plate. There was no firewood in the fireplace. But these must wait. If he didn't perform his professional duties, he knew, he would be fined. He had been fined eight times in his whole career as a town crier. It was not a pleasant memory, those fines, those stupid-looking old men, intensely looking at him, their gullets racing up and down in anticipation of the drink they would get from him. Especially Topa, his head like a Kuli water pot, and eyes flaming like a parrot's tail feather. Never did an honest day's work. All he knew was to sit in judgment on others and get a drink out of them.

He took his khaki trousers and the army bush shirt he wore every day down from where they hung on a wooden peg on the mud wall. When he lifted the trousers up, a small mouse rushed out. It raced for the thatch; and Kodzo cursed its ancestors swiftly.

The bush shirt was now grey with age and parts of the thread were coming out. The man who sold it to him said he was in the German war in Togo and Abyssinia. In the Great War against the Kaiser in 1914. So the shirt must be preserved. Kodzo Dzide now claimed that he himself was in the war. He talked after long bouts of palm wine at wake keepings of how he was on his way to Dahomey to consult fetish at Abomey; there they have the best fetish in the whole land; how he was arrested and beaten by the German governor called Herr Commandant, and later by a group of soldiers for refusing to carry their army haversacks. He didn't go to the war front anyway. He had a bad cough on his chest that year.

Then he remembered. The message that he was to announce to the Deme. Mr Attipoe's sister Dzenawo has brought forth a male child. Deme should know.

He went into his bedroom and stretched his right hand under the bed. There still must be something left in the bottle. His stomach had trumpeted again, this time as if a dog had delivered puppies there; she growled angrily at anyone who came near. It was his hernia which was going to be his death. There was a pock-marked Tongu medicine peddler who tried to cure him. He gave him all kinds of potions from his old medicine gallon. When he went one day for more the man was double bent grinding his testicles with his two palms. The medicine man couldn't speak. He was in the grip of hernia. Since that day Kodzo hadn't cared about his hernia any longer. If it was going to kill him, let it kill him.

He found the bottle in the dark, and lifted it eagerly to his lips. He spewed out what he drank. Kerosene. He found the second bottle. This time he smelled it. He took a long pull that coursed down his throat like fire. As the flaming liquid reached his stomach, it exploded in an angry snarl like the new mother bitch; then it subsided. The dog is quiet now, he said.

He unhooked his gong from the bamboo shelf near the fireplace and headed for the fig tree in Ablome to tell his message.

That morning was the eighth day. Dzenawo's son was to be outdoored. Anakpo, the leader of the family cult house, opened the fetish hut at the second cock. His cloth around his loins, he poured the drink offering. Then he called the gods, the ancestors, Mamagbo, Ashiagbor, Atitsogbui, Letsu, Wotodzo, Afedomeshie, Nyidevu, every illustrious man and woman of the household who had gone beyond.

> Take this child. He is your own child.
> Look after him. Be fire above his head.
> Guide his feet in this wilderness called life.
> Guide his feet, our fathers; guide him safely.

The same day, the circumcision was performed. His father, Jonathan, the postmaster of the village of Penyie three miles away, had insisted. It was what his clan of Batawo had demanded.

The pledge was made to the ancestors and the gods. The child should be their torchbearer and servant all his life. Neighbours came and looked at the baby. His father had left earlier to open the post office at Penyie lest his boss from Keta should come on inspection. Mr Attipoe sat in the middle and deputized for the father. Everybody said the child resembled his grandfather, Nyidevu, a man of the past now. He was a tree on which they all leaned, and under whose shade they all took shelter. Nyidevu, the canoe-upturning hippo, the hippos of Agave tried to upturn the canoes heaped with sand. Their necks snapped in the attempt.

Little one, take after your ancestor.
Take after him, live and grow grey hairs
on your teeth.

The child sneezed when a green herb wrapped in a cloth was rubbed on his forehead.

Ehe, he has responded.
He has responded. It is good.
It is indeed good.

Amamu they called him, the rum name of his great-grandfather. The man has fallen, do not help him to rise; if he rises, he rises against you.

## ••• Chapter 1a

Palm fronds, dried banana leaves, the devotees have taken to the forest. Someone has offended Yewe. Dalosu, he who conquers forests, and days, conquers nights. Seven nights they are in the forest, seven days they are in hiding, in the cassava groves in line among stalwart mangoes and silk-cotton seeds crackling, among distant baobab pods like breasts of pubertal virgins awaiting the ceremony of outdooring in the market-place, red flaming tails of parrots in their mouths. As buttock dimples rippled in silent ceremony high market lanes beads sapphire corals, sui adzagba sika stalked on their waists to abdomen. Seventh night at deep night when man's mouth has closed the law when they say the terrible god Sakpana will walk, sometimes covered with sores followed by barking dogs, sometimes the rich owner of land in velvet and a king's sandals shining on his feet dropping benevolence wherever he goes. The seventh night, deep deep night of the black black land of gods and deities they will come out. First the drums to-gu to-gu to-gu to to to-gu if they insist and say it must be by every means. If they insist then I shall die the death of blood I shall die the death of blood. They will march through every lane drums echoing across no one can tell where they are now, no one can tell. They will pause for entrance into thunderhouses the silence of crickets nocturnal wail of bullfrogs taking over from as near as Kosivi's ground water tank. If they insist insist and say it must be by every means, if they insist then I shall die the death of blood. The echo recedes into distant farmlands the sole witnesses of the journey the restlessness of gods if they insist if they say it must be by every means then I shall die the death of blood.

The flash point of creation, birth before birth long tunnels tunnels roads of womb darkness stilled the mind's eye cannot behold, prescience prenativity of total darkness, the foreknowledge of the grave the exhilaration and impatience of the emergence. Foetal passages palm tree harmattans dry dry in birthwaters of the rivers and the rivers swimming at the estuary the entrance to the sea. Penetration of a stalwart penis into the moistness of a vagina, the point being made in an ecstasy, legs thrown into a fit of urgency. And I was conceived in your image.

Dark, dark the grave's darkness sounds impenetrable in howling winds in infant eyes. They said I had the forehead of my grandfather, he who went empty-handed to war, the ear lobes of my great-uncle, and the arrogant mouth of my mother. They threw water upon me that morning at the edge of the eaves on the earth, on the dry presowing of yam holes covering in the fields. I do not know where they buried my birthcord.

Dark, dark the grave's darkness as ghosts walk in purple velvet provoking laughter from me by poking their fingers in my armpits and saying I believe he laughs he laughs when he laughs his penis gets up we are sure he wants a woman we bet he does want a woman. Clutching at globular breasts firm spring fountain nipples of raining milk cooing little little goat your mother is not at home your father is not at home for whom are you crying, who beat you little little goat spit in my palm and I will smack him for you little little one keep silent. Aunts they come to cuddle the infant; grandmother she carried firewood and corn and cassava to the birth house of an eldest daughter first grandchild with the forehead of the grandfather, the ear lobes of his great-uncle and the defiant mouth of his mother.

The benevolent ones demand we do their will. The holy ones of the shrines in the little hut on a back riding I went to them for the presentation. It was still dark, no longer the darkness of the primal tomb, the darkness of bright lights in which eyes open but cannot see, darkness peopled by ghosts in purple velvets shrieks abandoned by fireplaces by the eaves of the thatched hut in rain falling falling falling as the water whitened by cornflour is poured on the sogged earth for the benevolent ones to drink to quench their thirst in the land beyond the field where trees are green and the grove is dark.

The darkness of light lightens into wide dilating eyes the ghosts in purple velvet toss one from hand to hand and the cry whose child is that you are doing that to whose child tossing drawing the giggles of my infant laughter in the exhilaration of the darkness of the new light. Sometimes I rode on the back of one of the smaller ghosts gidiga gidiga, rode through centuries I cannot recall. Mother, didn't I tell you I hated the sun, father, didn't I tell you I hated the sun, the little one they searched for was never found they must journey to god's house and purchase him with offerings, must buy him with sacrifices look after him well, mother.

Darkness of night by glowing fires lit with flimsy twigs blazing in the distance of the tunnel womb of my beginning cracking in the coital moment of my creation. Voices are faint now, now loud sounds far away in the fields of the gods in the fields among the palms among the silk-cotton among the baobab in the distant farm-lands away. Bring a rag this child has passed excrement I don't know what is wrong with him these days it is not long ago he passed excrement.

Crawling after fevers running stomachs touching the fireplace with tiny fingers scream scream scream; you can't look after a child, if it were food you would be filling your stomach with it with double hands. Crawling, crawling picking up and eating tasteless chicken droppings, is there no one here and this child is eating chicken droppings. Crawling among long pots trying to stand by them that child is going to fall into a water-pot one of these days. Crawling to the cat grey eyes looking penetrating calm hands stretching to catch its eyes it moves quietly quietly away the cat is going to claw this child one of these days.

Standing and falling scream scream into mother's bosom, little little goat Mother is not at home Father is not at home for whom are you crying who hurt you cast a spit I will smack him for you little little goat.

Picking up sounds. Ghosts are real. Real. But they walk faster, erect, they run, they jump. The darkness deepens into light.

Bright bright days in the fields outside picking flowers catching rainbow-coloured butterflies in a wild garden. Chasing after the tangible ghosts in the fields I caught one. It was perched on a yellow sunflower wide as the moon. All colours of all hues. Serene. I caught it. He has caught it they screamed. That was my first catch. And the hunter is born in the butterfly field in the wild field of sunflowers.

Then it flew away. It would not rest where I held it gently in my palm it would not stay. It flew away. For days I searched the field looking for it. For days I did not see it. I saw others that looked like it. But no, it was not there. It is gone. The colours were different, its lines were different, its eyes were different. It is gone.

## ●●● *Chapter 2*

Did anyone see him pass? Did you see him?

Who?

Lawyer.

Which lawyer?

Perhaps he didn't see him; didn't recognize him. His personality can't escape notice for it is assertive and brutally distant. He was educated in England. And among the few who were educated abroad, he stands out for he is a brilliant lawyer and a gentleman. One P.M. Tuesday. The courts have just adjourned their morning session. A long line of lawyers, sweating freely in their black coats and their pin-stripe trousers, some struggling with their wigs and their black legal bags, are chatting animatedly as they descend the stairs through the Palladian pillars of the colonial edifice which now houses the Supreme Court of Accra. Following them, a host of clients, petitioners, litigants, pocket lawyers – case farmers, old men tired in their combat with the law, young men who have won a brief reprieve and have had their cases postponed. All listening intently to the lawyers. These brilliant children of our soil who have wrenched from the white man the magic of his wisdom. Their clients spoke in every tongue of the land. The lawyers inclined their heads gently to one side and listened to these men and women on whom their livelihoods depended as they strode towards their cars parked between the plots of zinnias, milkbushes and bougainvillea and the main road beyond which lay the sea.

Striding towards a grey Peugeot, and in the midst of a group of women and elders, was Amamu. He had had a busy morning. This was the end of a big land case which his client had just won against a European firm of diamond prospectors, Allen and Eliot. On his face was a grey look of satisfaction.

He was a tall man by all standards. Erect. He had a large head that was bushy with hair that rolled like a piece of disturbed black blanket. His eyes were deep brown, animated always, wise, and slightly cruel. His nose was rather long, made prominent by a slight ridge that separated the eyes and set them apart in a broad face. He sported a beard, now growing grey in parts, and joined by a finely trimmed line of bristly moustache.

He stopped by his car and had a few more words with one of the old men who bent his head towards the ground and listened intently to what he was saying. The old man nodded continuously, and nodded more. The lawyer reached for his briefcase and pulled out a piece of paper. This he gave to a young man, scarcely out of his teens, who stood behind the old man. His legal collar was loose now. He removed his black coat, folded it gently, put it at the back of the car, and eased himself into the driver's seat.

He drove away. The elders and the women turned round slowly and headed for the path between the milkbush hedges and the library towards the centre of the city.

Traffic was heavy. Especially traffic coming from the northern side of the city, from the centre near the banks and the shopping centres. He pulled up at the junction in patient anticipation of a lull that would enable him to turn left. He was patient. After a few minutes, he saw the lull he was waiting for. But he had misjudged the speed of the taxi from the centre of town. As he turned into the road, swinging left, tyres screeched, the taxi driver jammed on his brakes, eased opposite him, and said without venom or bitterness, Your mother's arse, don't you know how to drive? He drove on. He had heard what was said. It is part of the day's driving in the capital. He smiled a little smile and continued. The taxi sped on, horns hooting, and swung to the left near Parliament House.

By the time he reached the junction, the policeman on traffic duty raised his hand and stopped him. This was his regular traffic beat. He wore a sad face, like one who is burdened by the trials of life. He had no time for the luxury of a smile. It was they who were responsible. His face was arranged by his Maker that way. Sad, silent, as if enduring an internal agony irrespective of any gaiety around him.

He remembered this policeman distinctly. Five years ago. He went to court in Cape Coast. On his return just as he reached the outskirts of town, someone stopped him. It must have been a schoolboy.

Sir, your number plate is missing. The front one, the boy said. So he drove on towards his favourite fitter, a Peki man who had an open-air garage near the cemetery and charged moderate fees. On the ridge island near Second Avenue, the policeman stopped him. He stepped down from his signalling pedestal and came near the car.

Where is your number plate?

Oh, I just learned it's missing and . . .

So? And why haven't you fixed it?

I am on my way from Cape Coast.

But you could have fixed it.

How do I do it? I said I am on my way from . . .

But you could have tied it with a rope

That is a brilliantly stupid idea.

What, you talk to me like that? Bring your licence.

He pulled out his licence from his glove compartment, and gave it to the policeman. He studied it slowly. Then it all dawned on him. He was a lawyer.

Sir, I beg your pardon, sir, forgive, sir.

Next time be more careful.

Yes sir, lawyer, sir. Good-bye sir.

There he stood every day for these years on this pedestal which was the same throughout the city, going through the eternal marionette show of raising his hands, wheeling on his heels to stop traffic from Barnes Road, turning round to signal on traffic from Pagan Road. His face bore the same sad, lonely look, as if he had known no joy ever, as if he had never known laughter.

How are you, sir, master, today? No smile on his face.

Oh, I am fine. And you?

All correct, sir!

They had exchanged this greeting almost every day for the past five years. Then he realized how long a time it was since they first had their encounter. Why don't they ever promote this man? It was evident that he hadn't been promoted in five years. And he went through the same motions at his job year in year out, an eternal feature of the city streets.

The policeman signalled him on. He drove past the Institute of Arts and Culture where a crazy group of drummers and artists and their leaders were reviving African culture with a vengeance every day. On his left were the temporary buildings that housed the National Lotteries, a monument to the greed of men, erected to satisfy the money lust of the lowly workers of the city. Before the building was a huge billboard on which inexplicable numbers were posted every weekend by the hands of half hungry lottery girls legs like spindles in badly fitting clothes. Through the nim trees on the right, beyond the gullies carved out by many a rain, lies the ocean. Calm, beating ceaselessly on the sand. Under the nim trees, a few people were asleep. Some of the unemployed of the city. They slept here every day when the weather was good. On cardboards and cement papers they stretched their emaciated bodies, starved of food and joy for ages, while the surf that beat ceaselessly lulled them into fitful sleeps from which they woke up with a start at the least noise. There is no deep sleep ever for the poor. Near the next traffic light hurriedly erected a few years ago to give the city a modern look were the old colonial buildings that housed the Government Printer and the Public Works Department. Opposite, in similarly forgotten edifices, were the agriculturists, planning the nation's agronomical salvation from moth-eaten desks filthy with old tattered files. The planners were mostly old men who had risen up from the colonial service, and now E.O.s or S.E.O. with failing eyes, and a nagging and discomforting anxiety about how much their pensions and gratuities were going to amount to when they retired from the service. Beyond these buildings yet again among a set of old nims – colonialism in the Gold Coast was planted among nim trees – is another building which now houses the National Club. Built on stilts that are shaky, it is a wooden house that might have done service to a white colonial administrator who was in love with the Atlantic Ocean. In its rat-infested little rooms, shelves have been built to store drinkables. The kitchen now houses a bar, and the living room a billiard table. Here the senior civil servants return noon and evening, snatch a snack, and drink club beer.

He turned into the right lane when the lights changed into green. There were just a few cars under the nims. He locked the doors. A few thefts had been reported. He climbed the creaking wooden stairs.

Richard, the barman from Ijaw land in Nigeria, was at his post. A veritable servant, he had been a cook steward for years. When the club was formed a few years back, someone remembered having been served a drink by a servant with a smile in the house of one of the few white colonial civil servants who were still with the national government. So Richard got a job. Fifteen pounds a month, free housing – he lived in the cellar which was converted into a room with a bulb and a bed. At eleven every day he opened his little bar, checked the drinks, and the cash, and wrote everything in his bold slow hand into a small notebook provided by the committee. After that he perched half bottomly on the long stool behind the counter. From here he served drinks to his new masters, replied to polite and uninvolved inquiries about his and his family's health till late at night when his masters returned drunk to their suburban homes to their fat-arsed wives and spoiled children. Then he would descend into the converted cellar and eat his wife's cooking, and dream of his native land five hundred miles away in the creeks and the swamps of Nigeria.

Amamu was a little tired after climbing the wooden stairs. At thirty-five you begin to feel it, that youth is slipping away and you are winded and tired when you climb a short flight of stairs which you once bounced over as a young man.

A few of the club members were there drinking the ubiquitous club beer and chatting animatedly.

Hei, man, eh you look tired.

Well, it's been a terrible day.

What case was it?

It's that blasted land case from Oda.

Is it over? What's the outcome?

Well, we won.

A shout of joy greeted this news. Even Richard smiled from behind his little bar.

Man, let's celebrate.

Richard, bring four bottles.

Four bottles of well-frozen club beer were produced by Richard on silent feet. He never wore shoes. The glasses were filled and heads were thrown back in the act of thirst quenching. An act of libation.

Good, man. How did it go?

The man who asked the question was Alex. He had just been promoted Principal Secretary in the Ministry of Agriculture. He was a greying man of forty-five. Short and fat around the belly, he joined the service as a junior clerk twenty-five years ago. Through sheer doggedness he had pushed his way to the top. He studied hard, passed all the civil service routine examinations and had arrived at where he was. He talked a rather stilted kind of English, and when involved in an argument would produce sharp agricultural statistics and use agricultural terminology like any expert. Of course he hadn't been in the Ministry of Agriculture long. But he learned quickly. His greatest virtue was his self-confidence which he exuded in impatient remarks about university-trained men who thought they knew everything.

Near him, wiping his pair of glasses feverishly, sat Bob. Bob began life as a scientist in one of the first technical colleges established by the colonial administration. He was interested in physics, and still talked about experiments and test tubes. By some incomprehensible turn of fortune, he ended up a banker. He worked with the nation's leading banking institution in the city, after years in the service of a foreign bank for dominions and colonies overseas. Bob was a genial man, with an infinite capacity for tomfoolery. This had marked him out as a comedian and a great entertainer. A round man, athletic and bouncing, he fought against old age by running around on a tennis court every day, in the belief that a sound mind rested in a sound body. Apart from being a buffoon and a clown, he had the reputation of being a great ladies' man. Most of his jokes were about women's private parts, a subject he claimed to have been acquainted with, scientifically, since he was a ten-year-old boy at a school somewhere up country.

In a medium state of intoxication sat Row. Old Row was a police officer. Plain clothes. He had not been seen in uniform lately. He was a shy little man, with a stoop, and a flamingly red moustache. He had escaped being an albino just by a little miss of God's red paint. By ten o'clock every day, Row had been known to be incoherently drunk for many years. Nobody knew what he did at Police Headquarters. After his round of police duties in various towns across the country, towns in each of which rumour had it that he assiduously fathered a child or two, fate pushed him back to the capital. He was now at Headquarters where he was reported to be an assistant commissioner. Behind old Row lay a career of police intrigue, pursuit of criminals, coverage of agitators, and years of devoted duty to the colonial service. When the nationalists took over, old Row was at his post dutiful and ready to salute the agitators he had tracked down through blind alleys and slum dwellings of Takoradi and Sekondi, a few years back. Before him loomed a good pension and gratuity. His days, everyone said, were over. In fact, they said, that was why he drank.

Amamu had brought his coat from the back of his car. As he stood wondering where to hang it, Richard came forward and took it.

Now, let's have a drink, said Row, who could hardly keep his eyes open, as he belched palm nut soup and fufu.

How did it go? Bob asked.

That blasted firm is a nest of criminals. I don't know how they do it. And our government sits mum and doesn't say a word.

What do you think they should do? Alex asked a little vexedly. He had always resented lawyers and their airs.

Pass a bill reviewing the issue of mineral concessions, said Amamu without being convinced about the possibility of this happening himself.

Hmm. It was Bob, changing his voice into a whisper. He added, Don't you know why they can't do it? Chop some make I chop some. They collect from them; the ministers collect. I hear the big man himself is inside.

Old Row belched rather loudly. Is that so? he asked.

As for you, Row, you behave as if you don't know. Are you not a policeman?

How I go know. As for me I be ordinary policeman O. He meant he didn't want any trouble, his pension and gratuity were coming, and he would have a long booze till death called him. There was a comradeship among them which was deep, the absence of even the remotest possibility of betrayal.

But they can introduce legislation. It was Amamu. The law as it stands now is hopelessly inadequate; it offers no protection to the ordinary village people, and the stool families whose ancestors signed away acres of diamond land for a rent of one pound a year! It is criminal. With that he raised up his glass as if in toast to the descendants of those stupid ancestors who had just put a good deal of money in his purse.

Then they go about talking about socialism, Bob said. He raised his head and surveyed the nims, looked at his friends, took off his glasses, began to wipe them, and with a fierce finality added, Socialism their mothers' vagina. At this Alex roared hilariously. Not capable of coarseness himself, he enjoyed listening to and relishing it from other lips. So long as it was not his lips that said those vulgar words. But it was true. What Bob said. Socialism their mothers' vaginas. He said this in his head. Bob should have added *s* however, since their mothers didn't have only one vagina.

It was obvious that none of the group was going back to work that afternoon. Alex had had a meeting all morning. He was with his Minister. He could take the afternoon off. Oh, why? Man was tired. It wasn't his father's business. Old Row had spent the morning investigating a notorious diamond smuggler who was caught trying to bribe one of his inspectors. He had interrogated him all morning; ended up by going with him to have a drink in the man's house. But he must bring a case against him, his docket must be closed. It was rumoured that the man saw the COP frequently. He would be firm. But the Dimple Haig whisky was good. Yeah! It ran down your throat like water down a duck's back. Smooth, and fine, and mellow. That's the word, mellow. He'd closed for the day because he was tired.

A few more club members started to drift in. Some in tennis outfit, others in their working clothes. Tables were added to the already existing ones, as no one wanted to miss Bob's witticisms.

The newcomers included principal secretaries, high court judges, editors of national dailies, one or two army officers, senior African employees of foreign concerns, education officers. There were no women among them. The career women avoided the club like the plague, because they said it was a den of iniquity, where teen-age girls were enticed and raped in secret rooms by men old enough to be their fathers. This was not true. Now and then a man trailed in a pickup, or a nervous-looking undernourished girl who had appeared in his office looking for a job. The girl would sit, conscious of her spindly legs, and nervously drink a glass of beer, and would not say a word the whole afternoon because she was intimidated by the company.

The story is told of the wife of one of the principal secretaries, a Cape Coast woman who one day stormed the club. It was reported to her that her husband went there with a certain half-caste girl from his ministry. She had received several of these reports from friends and well-wishers in her husband's ministry. One lonely dreamy evening she decided to put a stop to the whole nonsense. At about 7.15 p.m. she jumped into a taxi and asked the driver to drive to the club. The taxi parked under the nims. She asked the driver to wait. She went round the building and took a look from the darkness of the awning at the balcony where the members sat. Her husband was there. Near him sat the half-caste girl. His fingers were playing a gentle rhythm on the girl's left leg, as conversation flowed. Oh, God, the things she heard. Filthy talk worthy only of street boys. And there sat all these big men shamelessly mouthing foul language at the top of their voices. She boiled for about three minutes. No. She must go away. Pretend she didn't see. She didn't hear. Then her husband's left arm darted forward and cupped the girl's right breast, and she, the whore, the daughter of a whore, laughed a shrill laugh. The laughter of a whore. At this the men laughed. Her husband, encouraged, turned round and held the girl in a lewd embrace. Oh, my gods, my fathers. Like lightning she had flown over the creaky stairs. No one knew how she came, where she came from. All that was heard was a sudden shrill sound, a wailing,

Ao Yehovah, help me.

She had made straight for the girl's throat. With her nails and her teeth she fell upon her. Her husband, a man of few words, and very respectable, was caught unawares. He reeled under the impact, as the two women grappled with each other. His chair had fallen backwards, and he himself was half thrown down. Meanwhile, almost everybody who was in the club that day had joined the melee in an attempt to end the brawl. The two outraged women were screaming obscenities as they writhed in a wild tangle on the wooden floor clawing at each other like civet cats. A few of the men who had gone to separate the combatants did so out of a malicious masculine desire to behold exposed tits with the expectation of more beyond.

When the women were finally separated, the fair-coloured girl from the ministry was half naked. Her pink low-cut dress had been ripped into two, one half hanging from the sleeve, as she tried desperately to hold on to the other half on her right shoulder. In the commotion, somebody had knocked off Bob's pair of glasses. He was running up and down the wooden stairs in a great state of agitation screaming: My spectacles, my spectacles! Has anyone seen my spectacles? No one was paying attention because the women had swung into a verbal match in which they hurled all kinds of abuses and slanders at each other. They named whose mother was a whore, a witch, a thief, who was a prostitute, and a dirty slut, who stank. Meanwhile, a car was pulling out of the nim trees, gears grinding. It was the Principal Secretary. He had sneaked off during the commotion after having lifted himself up with the help of Richard.

But that was some months ago. The Principal Secretary had stopped coming to the club, the story had grown stale, and everyone who wanted to bring a girl there thought twice.

Conversation flowed on. Amamu was leafing through a book he was holding. He had suddenly withdrawn from the discussion. His friends and the other club members were aware of this habit of sudden withdrawal. And they said he was a queer man. He also had a habit of introducing such outlandish topics as philosophy and theosophy. Whenever he read a book, he would come to the club talking about it. Last week it was Descartes. Some weeks ago he was on about Djilas' *The New Class*. Whenever he launched into these learned monologues, his friends listened with a shy deference, and admired his learning, but said to themselves: The man is mad. He would go on and on. Suddenly he would realize that no one said anything, no one interrupted. So he would become silent, withdrawal was his immediate refuge. Then he would gaze away to sea, his mind wandering away. After a while, his friends would pick up their conversation which had been interrupted. The voices would float around him. Suddenly he would call Richard and ask for his bill. And without a word to his comrades, he would descend the creaky stairway and drive away into the evening. They would all say he was mad. But very learned.

Right now he was thinking about a phrase used in court that day. He couldn't remember who used it. But it came out like a hanging spider's web in tangles over his vision. He was trying desperately to catch it and pin it down. But the wind blew it. If the spider were in it, it would be easier to get hold of the annoyance and remove it, destroy it. It dangled, the phrase. Was it 'the ignorance of the learned'? The ignorance of the learned. He had known a Ghanaian boy who spent five years in England learning Old English and Transformational Grammar. A few friends he had known had had glittering careers at Oxford studying Herodotus. The ignorance of the learned. It didn't sound like it.

He must go. Richard, my bill. The bill settled, he picked up his briefcase and descended the stairs. The others had stopped talking to watch him go.

The evening had come with the suddenness that it does in the tropics. There is the hour when the sun is red, like a broken oil pot over the sea, the clouds drifting aimlessly over the sea, and sea gulls in formation racing along the shore line northwards. Then the brief grey twilight which dissolves as quickly as it comes into montages of shadowy figures, shadows, colourless formations which again dissolve into the dark tropical night.

He emerged from the yellow bulb of the club into the darkness among the nims towards his car. A few bats were crying in the tree. They had dropped nim seeds on his bonnet. A few yellow leaves had also been blown on to the roof of the car.

He rolled down the glass near him. When he emerged from the darkness he noticed that the street lights had been lit. He turned right towards Osu. They had not lit the lights near the Independence Monument, and Black Star Square was black. Only the glimmer of the sulphur from the sea could be seen rising gently as it enveloped a few shadowy figures that were walking upon the beach two by two.

He paused for traffic from the right. There was none. But he always paused as the sign says, Give Way to Traffic on Your

Right. At the end of the long road on the right lined with coconut trees stood the old Castle. Lights were blazing from it as if it was on fire. Guards could be seen near the gate, holding on to their rifles. This was the seat of government. And the Leader, they said, slept there now and again. Some said he had bought a submarine which was all set ready to go through a tunnel that led into the sea in order to escape when the revolution came. It was, they said, an improvement on the same tunnel through which the slaves were shipped in ancient days (they were taken through the tunnel to prevent their being rescued by their families). In little boats they rowed in to collect their cargo of black ivory. Then they rowed to sea to where the ships were anchored, and tears and supplications were heard until they vanished into the horizon on their long journey to the Americas.

Traffic on the main Osu road was heavy. When he reached the T junction where he had to turn, it had thinned.

He pulled up near the forgotten refuse dump where he normally parked his car. He locked the doors, checked whether they were locked, and walked towards an old building which sat squatly on the corner where the women roasted pig.

He knocked on a door painted in a dim blue. It opened. It closed behind him.

## ●●● *Chapter 2a*

Bricks cement mortars pounding. A nation is building. Fart-filled respectable people toiling in moth-eaten files to continue where the colonialists and imperialists left off.

The poor are sleeping the sleep of the hungry under the nims. Benevolent one, thou who hast asked us to do your bidding, thou who hast begged us with tears in your eyes and soot on your face, Follow my laws, my children, follow my laws for I am the one who brought you from the dust of degradation.

And he cast us back into degradation. With the rage of the elements and the dissonant cry of mortars from saladins he cast us into the degradation. With the cry of Long live the Party, the Party is supreme, he cast us into degradation.

Woman, behold thy son; son, behold thy mother. This revolting malevolence is thy mother. She begat thee from her womb after a pregnancy of a hundred and thirteen years. She begat thee after a long parturition she begat you into her dust, and you woke up after the eighth day screaming on a dunghill.

You crawl through the dunghill of Nima unto the blue hills of smoke to catch the infinite immeasurable bliss to say to the dancers on the hills of spice, Lift up your cloths for the nation is yours, the land has come back. The yoke has been smashed by the knights of valour, the corridors are cleared for new feet to walk through.

Then they grasped the strength and energy and freedom of spirit not to make the infinite movement of resignation but to make the paraclete their own, to make the fire their own, to make the tongues that descended upon them that dark night lit by torches from a million and a million hands their own.

In the hush hour of birth came the songs, the sirens of joy and the land took on new colour, as voices raised a new chorus to the sky.

And no one stood alone in that hour. Strangers hugged one another, those who spoke not the same tongue embraced one another in the magic hour of faith and renewal of faith.

I am able by my own strength to renounce everything, and then to find peace and repose in pain.

The agony of Christ in Gethsemane after the denials, after the cup refused to pass away; return the miracle, return the miracle in the noon angelus, in the missal hour, in the throbbing vibration of ancient drums, husago, atrikpui; but let us return to the magic hour of our birth for which we mourn.

Crowds came from every corner of the earth. The feast of oneness is here. They raised a shout to the sky, to the heavens, like the Israelites of old they have arrived on the shores of a promised land, like the Anlo sojourners they have come to a place of sunshine, of water, of fish and of good things of earth abundantly given, they must roll their mats and go no more. They have come home.

Home is my desolation, home is my anguish, home is my drink of hyssop and tears. Where is home?

My search for a repose in pain is not an act of faith. It is an act of worship for fallen gods, gods burned out by colonial district commissioners armed with a governor's order-in-council: that all false gods among the pagan Gold Coast African should be destroyed; troops – an adequate number in order not to provoke uprisings and only where persuasion fails – destroy gods by persuasion – may be deployed with maximum precaution.

Our Father who art in heaven, do whatever pleases you. The menace of a raging tooth is eliminated by extraction, if necessary by force of arms meaning by persuasion.

So gods must be exiled, driven out of the land for failure, wicked unwarrantable failure. We had placed our hopes in them. They failed. They must go into exile. We don't care where. But they must leave the land which they have desecrated with their foul excrement.

Quis loquetur potentias Domini; auditas faciet omnes laudes ejus?

From the Palladian pillars we emerge, the greedy bastards of a new-found land. Who shall tell indeed the mighty deeds of the Lord?

Despair and die.

The self-illumination that comes of the losing of senses in a twilight field of new sensations and a new physical dimension will provide the avenue of final immersion, of the incessant and immutable necessity to be aware of our strength. Then, and only then, shall we assume the strength of lions, and stalk the spoor of him our Maker among the Creator's ignoble herd.

At a Party rally the other day, a man led the gathering in prayer for prosperity, long life for the Leader, safety for all, and proceeded to compile a list, with the help of Party activists from corporations of those who are known to be anti-Party, and must be detained so that the Party and the Leader must remain forever. Then they sang a hymn, 'Lead Kindly Light Amidst the Encircling Gloom, Lead Thou Me On'. This was ended with the Party anthem, 'There Is Victory for Us'.

Three days after, the anti-Party elements were flung into the maximum security prison in Nsawam.

After the firing of the muskets on the famous twenty-fourth, the Party activists were rounded up. Some were screaming in tears and supplication, some marched with their beads bowed. Then they were beaten, on television only. They were not beaten in reality. The world was told it was a bloodless take-over. Some women have not seen their husbands since, except those who saw their husbands since in army uniforms driving Mercedes 250 top speed towards the Castle. The same Castle where the slave ship anchored, and received their cargoes through the tunnels to the Americas.

I remember him limping into my office one day; his cousin had been accused of stealing Coca-Cola money. Would I take the case? The amount involved was £37 18s. 9d. A man must not go to jail for such a paltry sum. It is an execrable shame.

On the Liberty Arch the words are inscribed, 'Freedom and Justice'. The darkness of the black star lies in its square where immense appropriations are made to increase the striking force of the army of a starving, naked and diseased nation to march and wear its boots newly received from England under certificates of urgency – judging the state of depletion of the national coffers – the one who left stole all the money, the bastard, the b.f. – new epaulettes, new strings, new crowns for newly appointed generals and brigadiers, and uniforms for latrine carriers.

Fear death by guns.

A timore inimici eripe animam meam.

## ••• *Chapter 3*

Deme Primary School in 1936 was not a very peculiar school. It was built by the Roman Catholic missionaries who came long after their rivals in Christ the Methodists had built their church on a small hill. Then came the Presbyterians. These churches flourished together in the word of God, nourishing their priests on the crops of the farms and fish from the Aka River.

The school was not separated from the church. The instructions included writing, reading and arithmetic, the three Rs. The most important subject however was catechism. Instructions in these subjects were brisk and accompanied by the rod. They were conducted by cheerless old men who were scarcely literate, but who understood and had received the calling.

Class stand!

Good morning, sir.

Good morning, children.

Sit down.

Kofi Alakpa.

Present, sir.

Yao Avugla.

Present, sir.

Florence Dodzavudzi.

Absent.

Why? I am sure her mother has brought forth another baby.

Who said that?

Tsitsa it is me.

I've taught you not to say, It is me. Give him a knock on the head, the boy nearest him. Fine.

What should you say?

It is I.

Good, next time don't forget, you silly goat, hopeless cow.

Class stand, sit, stand, sit.

After the drill intended to keep the children awake the teacher cleared his throat.

Now, catechism!

This was a favourite subject. Those from Christian homes liked it. It was those children whose parents were pagans and heathens who didn't feel comfortable with the subject.

Who made you? You.

Silence.

He doesn't know it. Keep standing.

Next!

God made me.

Why did God make you? Next!

He made me so that I do His will here and go to serve Him in heaven.

What are the sacraments? Next!

Baptism, Confession, Communion, eh, eh, eh.

He doesn't know it. Keep standing.

What are the holy sacraments? Next. Next. Next.

All right. All those who failed to answer questions, fall out. Then a bundle of well-cut canes would be brought out by the class prefect. And the laggards would have six lashes on their backs.

The bell would ring for recreation. This was the time all the children waited for. Those who had coppers would rush to the women who sold beans, gari, rice and stew. And many other delicious foods. Those who didn't have coppers would go begging with cupped hands.

Give me some or your mother will have a baby with crooked hands. Then they would collect rice, beans, palaver sauce, abolo in their cupped hands and retire behind the big nim tree on the compound and eat.

These were the children who were not properly trained at home. Those who had received good training at home but didn't get morning coppers came to school with either roasted corn or gari and a cube of sugar in their pockets. When the bell rang for recreation, they retired behind the school latrine and scooped corn or gari into their mouths. When they finished their meals they rushed to the women sellers for water to drink. Sometimes they were given. Sometimes they were not given.

The following year, the school got permission to establish a senior school. This was after the Inspector had visited the school, inspected the new classrooms built the previous year. It was completed because the children worked extra hard cutting bricks, fetching water, collecting and selling firewood, thatch, and mats to pay the bricklayers and to purchase roofing sheets from the local U.A.C. store by the market.

Mr Smith, the School Inspector, visited the school a term after the senior school had opened. He went to Cambridge University where he got a fourth in history, ancient history. He was young, twenty-two, and energetic. His prospects in the colonial education service were bright. This was his second year in Africa. He lived in Keta, in a big bungalow by the sea with four servants – a cook, a steward boy, a driver, and a night watchman whom he always suspected of being a thief. He wrote home regularly to his mother in a village in Suffolk. He wrote home about the beauty of the country, of the natives, how eager they were to have education, well, some of them. But he could not stand the infernal night drumming that they carried on. He was learning about the customs of the tribes, particularly that of the area in which he was called upon to work. They worship thunder! They have native schools, seminaries one may call them, where they produce young cult priests every year. He had seen their processions in town, a weird affair in which young initiates danced the whole day to the point of physical exhaustion.

To him, the concept of the white man's burden was vague, undefined. He saw it in terms of a well-paid job, a good house, and a vision of arriving at the top – if the Empire was still there. Of course nothing can happen to the good old Empire. He wrote regularly to Susan. They met in Cambridge. He hadn't had the courage to propose to her yet. But it would come.

When Mr Smith stepped out of his official motor-car at Deme one morning, Mr Agbodzan, the head teacher of the Roman Catholic School, was ordering the removal of all canes from the classrooms. He had not been to a Teacher Training College. But he had got to the top through sheer will power and hard work. His favourite maxim was, 'Brighten the corner where you are.' Brighten the corner where you are, my boys.

When the Teacher Training College at Hohoe was opened he was too old to pass the entrance examination. But he held the External Certificate. Almost every year Mr Agbodzan vanished to Accra to sit for London Matriculation. After the eighth attempt, the children had made up the story that he was told by the examination people in the capital not to come again. If he did they would write a letter to his Education Circuit head. So he stopped going to sit for the London Matriculation in unheard-of subjects like algebra, geometry, trigonometry, and some said Latin was included.

He was an interpreter at church on Sundays, especially on great feast days, like the feast of the patron saints Peter and Paul. His white drill suit would be well starched and ironed, his hair cut, and he would wear a black tie which he bought at a Conference of Headmasters at St Augustine's College in Cape Coast many years ago. He would anticipate every move of Father James, and move silently to join him at the foot of the altar to listen and interpret the word of God.

He was a respected member of the community. People brought cases to him to judge because he possessed both the wisdom of his fathers and the white man's wisdom.

Tall, well built, bald, he was a disciplinarian who ruled his household with an iron fist. Woe betide any boy who was brought up before him for a major breach of a serious school regulation. He ruled the school with a fervent lay preacher voice, and a bundle of twelve well-cut canes behind his cupboard in his office.

Mr Agbodzan walked up nervously and offered his hand to Mr Smith, the Inspector of Schools, Keta District. Mr Smith ignored the offered hand. He could not afford the luxury of personal intimacies. These fellows must be put in their places.

Good morning, Mr Smith, I hope you had a good ride. Our roads are bad, sir.

Good morning. Can I see the school logbook?

Yes, certainly, Mr Smith. In my office, sir!

The Headmaster strode ahead perspiring. Mr Smith, a short man, walked with the cocky dignity of the representative of the King and the Empire in the field of education.

The logbook was duly inspected, and Mr Smith wrote in it with red ink.

Can I see a class in session, Mr Headmaster?

Yes, certainly, Mr Smith. Class Five, sir.

Can I go into class Four?

The Headmaster was not prepared for this. He had had class Five prepared for inspection because Mr Kwawu, the class Five teacher, was a reliable old teacher who knew how to teach and who understood discipline. Mr Adama, the new teacher in class Four, was merely a boy, a product of the new Training College, inexperienced. More sweat poured down his face.

Class stand! Class, this is the Inspector of Schools, Mr Smith.

Good morning, master, good morning, sir! chanted the children.

Will you continue the lesson, Mr Adama? Inspector would like to observe the class in session.

This was Mr Adama's first year as a teacher. He had been taken unawares. How could the Headmaster do this to him? Adama twitched his mouth, brought out a large red handkerchief and wiped his face.

Before you continue, may I see the class register?

Yes, sir.

Mr Smith looked into the register perfunctorily and signed the day's page in red ink.

You can continue the class.

Yes, sir.

Class stand, sit, stand, sit.

After the drill, Mr Adama cleared his throat, his heart in his mouth.

What insect carries malaria fever?

Several of the children who would normally have put up their hands did not because they were afraid. One tiny boy in the front row whose nose was always running put up his hand timidly, and a small voice a little louder than a whisper said, Tsetse fly.

Wrong, next!

Mosquito.

Yes, which mosquito?

Anopheles.

Good. Now. Who discovered disease germs? You, Kofi Alakpa.

George Stevenson.

Wrong, next!

Florence Nightingale.

Wrong, next! Mr Adama was becoming desperate. He was drenched in sweat. His handkerchief hung limply from his shirt pocket where he had nervously stuffed it.

Next!

Louis Pasteur.

A little smile played on Mr Smith's face. He paced the classroom slowly in between the desks and eyed the children with the mischievous twinkle of a censorious uncle.

Class stand! Sit, stand! Sit.

The inspection was over. Mr Smith wrote in Mr Adama's teaching notebook in red ink. As he stepped out, the class like one man stood.

He stepped out into the morning sun, and lit a cigarette. Mr Agbodzan followed him to his car. The School Inspector sat at the back and said, Good morning.

Good morning, sir, safe safe journey, sir.

The school breathed again. Mr Agbodzan was annoyed. He was very angry.

And I am older than him, am I his co-equal? he muttered, addressing no one in particular. What is this? Eh? He will write his report and it will severely go against the school. And me.

That day Deme Roman Catholic School went into mourning. Teachers caned whole classes on the slightest provocation and pretext. Old offences were dug up and the appropriate lashes administered promptly. Those who had missed church service about three weeks previously and had even forgotten about it were put on the backs of stalwart boys from the villages, and whipped like dogs. No one in class Four got away that day. It was a weary day of loud noises, of lashes, of screams, tears and no joy. A few of the little ones pissed in their clothes, and they had to find rags to wipe the urine from the floor. As they searched for rags they rubbed their buttocks with their left hand and strove to wipe tears away with their right hand. It was a weary day.

Mr Agbodzan, the Headmaster, was very angry. He called a hasty staff meeting in his office.

Gentlemen, he said, concentrating his gaze on Mr Adama, you are all capable of guessing Mr Smith's report. It is bound to be adverse. And the responsibility of answering before the General Manager falls squarely – he loved the expression 'falls squarely' – on my shoulders. Yes, on my shoulders. He paused with the emphasis on the words staring venomously at Mr Adama.

What shall we do? Yes, gentlemen. What shall we do? His voice collapsed in a near whisper, a sudden giving up, a submission overcame him. He turned round, pulled his chair and sat down. The staff sat glum, silent, utterly lost.

The history of colonial education is one long war between the young and arrogant white school inspectors and the teachers. This was eventually brought to the mission that administered and ran a particular school. It was a sad dismal war in which the young pupils were caught, the veritable first victims of every first volley from the cannons of the pedagogues.

Mr Smith arrived home at Keta, tired and thirsty. His steward boy, Seidu, was faithfully standing in front of the house. The night watchman was squatting on the ground grinding his matchet chewing a long cane. Disgusting habits these natives have, chewing timber!

Seidu!

Sah!

I come. Cook make chop?

Yes sah, masa.

Any beer in the fridge?

No, masa. Masa Anginia come drink am. E bring some woman, they come drink all, masa.

It was Geoffrey Allen, the District Engineer. Degenerate and stupid, sleeping with native girls. That's what being here for too long does to you. You end up sleeping with native girls! He is an inveterate drunk and a fool. Washed up, that's what he is, washed up. You can't help liking the ass though. He was the spirit of every party. Has a lot of funny stories. Take that one he told about the driver of the night soil van who went on a one-man strike because he wanted a raise. Drove and parked the truck right in front of the Sanitary Inspector's office. Refused to move. He got his raise.

Mr Smith smiled at the joke, and Seidu, seeing that his master smiled, also smiled, relieved.

Seidu!

Sah!

Where dey cook?

Ah no know, sah. Look lak igo for im jolley house. That's what they are. They can't let their whoring women alone.

What chop he make?

Lam chop, sah.

Make table, Seidu.

Smith relaxed in his armchair. Seidu unlaced his shoes and brought him his bedroom slippers and a bottle of club ginger ale. The smell of food drifted into the room. He closed his eyes. And dreamed of England.

24th May, 1940. Empire Day. Birthday of Queen Victoria, the great English Queen under whose shadow and energetic supervision the British Empire was built. The Empire on which the sun never set.

The whole of Deme was gathered at the Victory Park. The brass bands from the three schools played the latest airs. The school children, well washed in their starched and ironed khaki shorts and shirts, stood in the blazing sun, miniature Union Jacks stuck in their shirt pockets waiting for the King's representative to come. They were waiting for the District Commissioner.

Empire Days were days the school children always looked forward to. They learned new songs that year. The new class Four teacher who was also the singing master had said he would make Deme Roman Catholic School the brightest example in the Empire. He taught many new songs to the school and the band that year. 'Some Talk of Alexander' was the most popular. They relearned 'Rule, Britannia' and 'Men of Harlech in the Hollow' and all the stanzas of 'God Save the King'.

The children stood in the blazing sun waiting for the great King's representative to arrive.

When Britain first, at heaven's command,
Arose from out the azure main,
This was the charter of the land,
And guardian angels sung the strain:
Rule, Britannia! Britannia rules the waves!
And Britons never never never shall be slaves.

They sang with gusto, relishing the martial fervour of the song and the knowledge that they too as Britons would never never never be slaves! Britannia rules the waves. Deme was among the waves, of heathen lands afar where thick darkness broodeth yet.

And Britons never never never shall be slaves. The grandeur of the refrain rolled through the whole of Deme. Those who went to their farms that day heard it. Infant voices from three schools asserted their Britishness far away from the benign eyes and ears of their great King. They were waiting for his representative.

Rule, Britannia, Britannia rules the waves, through the strong arms of asthmatic officials, adventurers, drunks, homosexuals, visionaries, and soldiers with booming drill ground voices and flashing moustaches. The men – and their women – who took formal possession of distant lands in the name of the King, fought in the name of the King and died in the name of the King so that the great Empire on which the sun never sets shall live a thousand years, nay, a million years.

Deme was sweating and waiting for His Majesty the King's representative to arrive. The school children, after a few lusty refrains of 'Rule, Britannia', swung into 'Some Talk of Alexander and Some of Hercules'. That day, they lumped together all great men. In the mystic valour of Hercules they saw Alexander – alas, he was Greek – Cecil Rhodes, Robert Clive and Lord Lugard, the eternals of colonial history.

With a tow row row row
To the British Grenadiers

Deme also sang of the valour of the British Grenadiers.

Half a league, half a league onwards. These men rode like the idiots of Balaclava, more than six hundred of them, they rode into the valley of death so that the great and mighty Empire on which the sun never sets shall forever live.

Mr Henry Douglas, the District Commissioner, was having breakfast. His official uniform had been well ironed the previous day. His plumes were all in order. If only the Governor didn't insist on reports about Empire Days, reports of how the King's loyal subjects received His Majesty's speech. The heat. The terrible heat. Mr Douglas had done eight Empire Days now and he drew nearer to higher office in the service, he hoped.

His wife, Mary, came into the dining room. You saw at once that she was a woman who had suffered long neglect. She wore a beautiful long floral dress. Harry bought it for her when they went on leave last year. She was a tall girl from a middle-class home fallen on evil days, very thin, with a face like a half-moon that the firmament had deliberately tilted to look funny to little children. Her nose was long, redeemed gently from turning hawkish by a pair of large eyes the colour of turquoise, calm as the lakes of her native homeland. She had a pair of animated full lips. On seeing her you concluded that the face was borrowed to fit on this thin lean and crumbling body. She hated being here. You saw that in her eyes. Her only hopes were woven around the three months' home leave in England when she would talk intelligently about Africa, the black nights, the comforts of the service and the natives who were perpetually drumming in the night. In England, her love for Henry blossomed like spring flowers after a hard winter. But she abhorred the way he dressed in England. They fell in love when she was working in a little coffee shop across from the Crystal Palace. She lived in Stockwell, caught the 37 every morning to climb the hills that were no more, to spend a dreary day five days a week for nine pounds ten. Henry was with the R.A.F. and had just been given his discharge papers because of his failing eyesight. Tall and jovial, he fell romantically in love with her at first sight. Her family, what was left of it, came from Cornwall, an aging mother suffering from acute arthritis. He came from Aberdeen. After a brief and hilarious courtship they got married in a small Presbyterian chapel in North London. Her people came and her mother shed a tear when it was announced that the newly-wed couple would go to Africa. From that day, her world had collapsed. He had never even hinted that he had joined the colonial service. Nor did she know that their honeymoon would be a hurried affair in Brighton. She wept most of the time on board the M.V. *Apapa* that took them to Africa. They landed at Takoradi and were met by a bunch of seedy-looking government officials. She had heard that the colonies turned people's heads. It made them funny. Eight years and her temper grew worse. She got farther and farther away from her husband. They never had a child. A child would have made all the difference in the world. A bouncing blue-eyed girl on whose head she would hang ribbons. The other women and their husbands looked so happy. She took to drinking to drown her intense loneliness, a drinking which was not heavy, a pathetic attempt at self-emulsion. Her husband grew more distant every day, absorbed in his work. They cast pitying glances at her. Whispers were in the air. He was sleeping with a black whore up country, they said.

Hello, Mary darling. I am sure Harry is gone on trek.

Darling Mary, Harry hasn't come back yet?

My dear Mary, you must miss Harry when he goes on his long treks. It was always Mrs Higgins, the Sanitary Superintendent's wife with the face like an owl's.

She felt oppressed, and dead. Her sex went to sleep. Then Gary Arnold came to Keta. He was with the police force. Young, energetic and devilishly handsome. He saw her; she felt he was lonely too. One long black night when Harry was away she invited him home to dinner. That night onwards, she began to live again, like a river awakened by the spring sun from a long sleep of a dismal winter. To feel Gary's strong military body in her tiny arms, to cry and to ache with the pain of joy whenever he took her. It was life. She went flower hunting on long afternoons with him in the car. Then they would sit under the shadow of the tall lighthouse at Woe, and watch the sun set over the Atlantic, and think together of England far away beyond the sea.

Then Gary went on leave. She waited for him, dreamed of him, and prayed that he should return safely. One day, word went round. Gary had returned, with a wife! A lovely kittenish thing with freckles and the laughter of a schoolgirl. Mary aged prematurely in a week. Her life had ended. Like the little leaf joying in the flood of spring until the river deposits it on a lonely bank, she had been deposited. But she kept her teeth together. She didn't cry. They said a wild look came into her eyes like the civet cat that has lost her children. She kept on. It must be so if Harry must keep his job; he had his African whore. And she had – nothing, not even a dream any more.

Are you ready, my dear?

Yes, I am. Can we go? The poor devils must be tired of waiting in the hot sun.

Time doesn't move in Africa, my dear. The chaps out there don't even know what time is. I've always told you.

The official car flying the Union Jack swung out of the District Commissioner's residence and started the thirty-mile drive to Deme. Mr Henry Douglas tapped his coat pocket to make sure the address was there. It was there. He remembered he must make a little informal speech after the parade at the reception organized by the chiefs and elders of the four villages. He had always needed three large whiskies to obscure the depressing demands of the informality of that occasion. He was at his best on platforms. The people then became distant and he read the address at them from the safety of the official dais. But the reception after was always an ordeal. He remembered one occasion, four years ago, when a petty chief let off a loud fart. Everybody turned round and looked at him. He tried desperately to hide his embarrassment for the poor man who stood barely four feet away from him. And the others behaved strangely, they kept their gazes on him as if expecting him to say something about the fart. When he inquired later about their behaviour from the local District Secretary, a loud-mouthed drunk with a dirty collar, he said it was known among his people that if you farted before a white man he would give you a gift of money. Incredible people, these Africans.

Meanwhile Deme and its surrounding villages waited for His Majesty's representative. Rule, Britannia, Britannia rules the waves. The chiefs and people were gathered. Some came out of curiosity. They had finished planting the May crop. So if the white man was coming to talk some nonsense about a King far away, they might as well go and hear. When the moon is shining don't cripples hunger for a race?

Some talk of Alexander and some of Hercules. The school children sang lustily for word had reached the gathering from the Boy Scouts posted three miles away that the District Commissioner was on his way.

Rule, Britannia, Britannia rules the waves.
And Britons never never never shall be SLAVES!!!

The black car swung in through the bamboo gates of Deme Victory Park. The policemen ran; one opened the door and Mr Douglas, O.B.E., D.C., stepped out followed by his wife, Mary. He stood at attention, the whole of Deme stood at attention. Old men removed their hats, chiefs removed their chewing sticks from their mouths. Everybody stood at attention, a still, silent attention.

God save our gracious King!
Long live our noble King!
God save the King!
Send him victorious,
Happy and glorious,
Long to reign over us.
God save the King!

Mr Douglas was the first to break the spell of the anthem, as he put his helmet back, plumes and all, and stepped forward in long neutral strides towards the official dais. The dais was gaily decorated with buntings and flags that fluttered in the May wind. The local contingent of Boy Scouts gave the yell. The elders put back their assorted headgear. The chiefs replaced their chewing sticks. The distinguished chieftains smiled to the District Commissioner while the women beamed friendship towards his wife who was called a lady. The one white woman they saw around who was not wrapped in long white clothes, and you did see her hair and her legs. Not like the convent sisters wrapped in yards of white cloth. The State Secretary of Deme Traditional Area bent over the District Commissioner and had a word with him. They say he is a very powerful man, he talks even with white men. The school children were restless; none of them were to break up the line. This was the instruction received before they left the school compound for the route march.

Mr Douglas began to sweat; he braced himself up to go through the ordeal, the ordeal of the speech from Buckingham Palace. 'God Save the King' was played as he rose from his seat. He paced up to the microphone and pulled out the speech.

Nananom, Ladies and Gentlemen, it is a great pleasure for me to present once again on this memorable occasion His Majesty's address to you.

Once more, we send you warm greetings, coupled with the earnest hope that the flame of loyalty to the Crown and of patriotic devotion to our world-wide Empire burns as brightly as ever in your hearts and lives. The spirit of service is above all, that which should animate today all those who belong to our British Commonwealth of Nations and who are proud of its traditions, its ideals and its incomparable mission upon earth. Such service includes the service of God, the service of the state, and service of our fellow men, particularly those of every race, colour, and creed who share our imperial heritage. Our British peoples are generously endowed with the priceless gift of freedom, just laws and mutual confidence which flows from unfettered democracy. But commensurate with our privileges is the greatness of our responsibility. Upon the courageous shouldering of those responsibilities depend the solidarity and integrity of the British Empire, and with it the future peace and prosperity of the world. Confronted with international enemies and misunderstandings, and widespread human tribulation and unrest, let us remain true to our traditions and ideals, prepared to follow with undaunted courage the path of duty, wherever it may lead. Never have the various parts of the Empire been more closely linked in fraternal affection, more solid in their sympathies, and more mutually trustful than they are today, and the whole human family have derived benefits from their mutual co-operation.

Let us above all hold fast to the anchorage of truth and righteousness. Let us each and all, young and old, this Empire Day, in face of a tendency in many lands to accept a lower standard of faith and conduct than that which hitherto guided the civilized world, bravely resolve to remain steadfastly loyal to the faith of our fathers and to those high principles upon which the British Empire has been built, and without which it cannot endure. To be true and worthy members of the Empire, we must maintain unshaken our faith in God, in the Empire and in ourselves. God bless you all.

Mr Douglas finished reading the address, and stood at attention. 'God Save the King' was played as usual off key by the combined-schools band. The Scouts gave the yell again. The State Secretary raised up his helmet and shouted three cheers for the king:

Hip! Hip! Hip!

Deme replied Hurray with a deafening cheer that reached the distant farms. Farmers paused in their hoeing of the field and looked back at their village, chuckled, and bent down to continue their work.

Then the State Secretary stepped forward to read the address on behalf of the chiefs and people. He had been writing it since April. He composed several speeches. He trusted his pen. But finally he gave it to O. M. D. Dawson, Licensed Letter Writer, Deme and Abroad, who gave it a final polish, and produced a beautifully typed script in which red and blue colours mixed to form especially the capital letters, the *hs*, *ts* and the *ds*.

He cleared his throat. And there was silence. He cast a look round, and bowed to the District Commissioner.

Our most highest and friendly District Commissioner, representative of King George of England, we welcome you to our village once more again on this auspicious occasion in honesty and humility. The words from our great King and father, George, have made us happy indeed, and we want to reply. Tell the great and most highest King of England, Colonies and Dominions that his words have also made us very very sorry because some people are making trouble for England and want to make war on the King. This was told us by the Reverend Father Bakers last Sunday. He said Hitler is planning a war. We don't agree to German people planning war. Father Bakers said it. He is sitting here among us. Anyone can ask him. We hear they want to come and take the young men to Accra to go to soldier. This is a serious matter. We shall send the elders to District Commissioner so that they can discuss this matter at dawn. Yes, this matter is a dawn matter. It is the matter for white people and elders. Most highest District Commissioner, tell the Governor at Accra to tell the King our father at England that we want water supply like the one Ho people have. We want a good market, and six latrines. Our people go to latrine in the bush. This is not good. We are happy to serve our noble and gracious King. God Save the King.

During this speech the elders who didn't understand a word of what their learned Secretary was saying nodded approval intermittently. When it was over, the elders said yes, they had a learned man indeed, a man who could speak for them, a man who knew the wisdom of the old white people. Not like the small boys nowadays who couldn't even read a telegram. Then they called his rum names among themselves, the river, not a common river roars, if it wasn't the sea then it must be the Mono. They shook hands on it and replaced their pipes and chewing sticks in their mouths.

Meanwhile the head teachers were organizing their schools for the march past. Every year, people decided which school won in turnout, uniforms and smartness. Each school tried its best, and boys whose school uniforms were torn or who were crippled in any way were not allowed in the line.

The school children marched past briskly, miniature Union Jacks stuck in their pockets.

Eyes right!

Eyes front!

The salute and the military slow-march filed past Mr Douglas, who stood at a smart attention, a whimsical smile playing about his mouth as he watched the loyal subjects of the Empire march past. After the schools, the Wolf Cubs, and the Boy Scouts came with their displays and yells proclaiming that they would do their best.

The parade over, the District Commissioner drove away. Everybody went home to prepare for the afternoon session of sports, games and physical display. There were to be races such as egg and spoon race, sack race, eating the bread race in which the children were timed and he who ate up a loaf of bread quickest won a prize of sixpence, followers up received threepence and penny.

This was Mr Tamakloe's day. He was the P.T. Master. It was rumoured that he was in the army at Takoradi, but left out of anger because the officer had abused his mother. After he fought the officer he came back home. When the school wanted someone to teach feet astride jump, he offered himself and was employed as P.T. Master at five pounds a month.

## ••• *Chapter 3a*

The long road begins from here, begins from the foetal tunnel and winds serpentine through the grass the river and the sun for a covenant is drawn never to be broken, an oath is sworn, the seeds of alligator pepper are eaten over the carcass of a chameleon, the changing never changing. The road winds through tomorrows, for there are no yesterdays, and tomorrows they are wiped away by tears in the eyes of orphans, in the eyes of widowed women in the eyes of husbands who lost their wives in childbirth in the convent where white sisters in long gowns administer ether and cut open wombs with a pair of sewing scissors.

Touchstones, billboards, boardings carrying illuminated messages proclaiming the covenant.

The birth was tedious the pangs were painful as the struggle unto death raged in the death chamber for the deliverance. Then silently the deliverance occurred in the hour of eternity in the missal hour of reading the rosary and journeying the stages of the cross. See here, here they arrested him, Judas is pointing his finger at him, and here, here he plants a kiss upon him my Saviour you were sold upon a kiss for thirty pieces of silver. Here, here, they brought him before Herod who said he knew nothing of such matters so unto Caesar must he go. Here, Pilate is washing his hands in an enamel basin with a red band as the multitude cried, Crucify him, crucify him, release unto us Barabbas. There, there, they bring the cross on the back of the black man from Africa, Joseph, and he bore it with a steady gaze for his Saviour and there he the Saviour carries his cross mounting the hill, sweat falling from his face, and blood from cudgel wounds falling upon the triangular leaves of heart on which they mingled till today in front of the small Church of St Peter and St Paul. There, he falls, my Lord falls, and they whipped him with whips.

> And they smote him on the head with a reed
> and did spit upon him, and bowing their
> knees worshipped him.

There he falls, he falls yet again, ten times he falls as though beneath a mortal wound, but he was not destined to die there; his journey must be complete. He must arrive in Golgotha. There, there they are giving him a drink in a sponge, a drink of wine and hyssop. He must drink it, for it is his, the cup cannot pass away.

My God, my God, why hast thou forsaken me?

and they said he was calling on Elias. And he cried with a loud voice:

Father, into thy hands I commend my spirit.

St Luke

Even he, in his divinity, makes a commendation of himself unto him his father who did forsake him. Unto his father who begat him from his loins in the foetal tunnel of the Holy Mary Mother of God Pray for Us Now and at the hour of Our Death.

Sancta Maria, ora pro nobis
Fuerunt mihi lacrimae meae panes die ac nocte
dum dicitur mihi per singulos dies. Ubi est Deus Tuus?

I lost him on the way to the gnawing fields of knowledge at where the devotees of Yewe were circling the baobab with pods like breasts of ancient virgins to proclaim the miracle hour of his coming down, to proclaim the epiphany of all deities.

Our Father, who art in heaven, do whatever pleases You. The incipient dawn of that beginning still hangs like a cloud of spider webs upon the okra-slicing knife used just now to give the cat a knock on the head. And our trail grows, muddying the lane to the ancient Aka River to fetch the river home that all may drink water. On the way a mile to the river we saw Zaccheus on the fig tree proclaiming he had given all his goods to the poor and one amongst us said, Let us cast our stones at him so that he discontinues such profanities.

But none amongst us could cast the first stone, for we had sins in us.

Zaccheus, come down from that tree, for today salvation

comes to your house. He came down and led us to the river. We put down our khaki shorts and shirts and swam in the muddy water. Then behold there stands my Father with a long cane threatening to break our necks if we didn't climb down from the back of the crocodile and carry our water pots home. In a long trail we marched through the grassland past the Great Ago palm red in fruit sniffing its smell with our wet noses airborne as he-goats as Father marched behind us like the warders marching prisoners to the District Commissioner's bungalow to weed and cut his grass in the luxuriant May month when the grass is green.

Then the District Commissioner came out with his dog, a tall huge creature like a horse, his nostrils breathing saliva as he jumped and played in the green grass off leash, as he jumped and on his hind legs licked his master's face. He is like the dog on H.M.V. records singing into a funnel large like our mother's which she uses to measure every drop of oil into bottles for the market day that falls on Sunday and we must miss church service. Father is swishing his cane among the grass as rats scatter to the four winds on hurrying feet, to the four winds they scatter as we huddle together from the cold of wet skins from the Aka River in this early cold May evening.

Give us a sign, they said. There shall be no sign given you except the sign of Jonah in the belly of the whale.

The District Commissioner and his dog vanished we know not where and my father's feet stamped stamped and his cane swished as on our wet backs when we continued the trail homewards.

We are almost home.

Then the canes fell on us with the venom of bees upset in the palm grove on wine pots newly collected sweet and intoxicating leading to brutal defecation on the compound of early dawn as the dew fell on my body. For Father said, Let no one allow him into the rooms. They lashed the canes lashed swiftly the tingling bite cutting my skin in sharp unyielding anger. And I broke my water pot. My people, I broke my water pot on the gravel path through the singing grass by the mighty Ago palm of a May evening returning from the river, returning from a ride on the back of the ancient crocodiles.

I heard the dog bark then. Clear and sharp like the report of guns from hunters at Iefo, from hunters vaulting over fallen tree trunks in the deep deep forest. I bend down to collect my broken water pot. The cane lashed again now sharper than the first and the dog barked a third time. And I knew my betrayal was over.

The silence of now is beyond words, beyond saying. It wounds the already wounded bark of my skin in a vengeful spite. I toss, toss for I missed the missal hour, I did not hear the noon angelus.

They were brothers. They had set traps in an anthill long deserted by the ants for bush rats, small rodents that feed on maize and ground nuts, others say wickedly also on a supplement of human flesh. That is why they are so good to eat. His, the elder's, trap caught nothing, as it caught a bush mouse which could scarcely provide a single meal; his, the younger's, trap caught a huge bush rat, big with eyes still staring as if pleading with the trap. The elder came first to inspect the traps. He saw his junior's trap had the good catch. And his trap caught the worthless little mouse which cannot provide a meal. Then it occurred to him. Suppose, suppose he took the mouse and placed it in his brother's trap, suppose, suppose he placed the bush rat in his trap. Then he bent forward. He was carrying out his plan. But his brother had climbed a tall tree and saw his brother exchanging the animals. Then he ran the run of deers and came. And clubbed his brother on the head to death. Dead for a mouse. He went home and had a feast. Whenever they asked, Where is your brother? he said, He is gone on a journey to Dahomey to consult fetish, every day they asked him he said, He must be on the way home from Dahomey where he went to consult fetish. Then one day a dog, it is always a dog, smelled the rotting carcass of an animal in an anthill. His master, the hunter, was following a spoor. He called his dog several times. It was not near. Then he went back. The dog was feasting on rotten entrails of a man whose nostrils and mouth and eyes were choked with houseflies – ordinary houseflies that you find in every home and in every market. They arrested the younger brother and placed the remainder of the carcass on his head. He must take it thirty miles on foot to the hospital in Keta for a post-mortem examination. After that they took him to Accra and hanged him for killing his brother for a mouse.

## ••• *Chapter 4*

He stepped into the dim light of the bed-sitter. The bed was loaded with clothes; at the head of it hung one of those new plastic wardrobes bulging with dresses. There were two armchairs covered in mauve. A centre table sat square between them. On it a glass vase with plastic flowers that were fading with time. In the corner near the first window was a dressing mirror locally made, tall with a small chest of drawers attached. Near the second window, iron-barred like the first to keep thieves away, was a round table on which sat a record player. One record was on the turntable covered with dust. The room had not been swept that day, the rug at the entrance was full of sand.

Holding the door was Adisa. A cloth wound around her, her breasts half showing; she was holding a tin of Bint el Sudan talcum powder. She had just finished her evening bath.

Eh. You are welcome.

Thank you.

He sat down and stretched his legs. Adisa put the powder on the table. She bent down. She started to unlace his shoes. She did this with a grace that was not of this world. She untied the laces gently with her long forefinger, raised his foot up – it was the left foot; she always started with the left foot – and proceeded to jerk it out of its hold. She turned round and gently pushed near the centre table. She placed his foot on it. She bent down and went through the same motions. She rose up after lifting the right foot on to the table. All that done, she raised up her head and looked into his eyes. He smiled, a small smile of gratitude and of love.

How was your day?

Oh, so so. And you?

I went to market and I cooked your favourite food.

Is that so?

It's a question, if it's a question, which he always asked. He never expected it to be answered. It never was.

She moved towards the record player. Underneath the table were records. She looked out for his record. She turned the first knob, and the turntable began to turn. It was a popular song those days. One of those sentimental love songs which even serious-minded people like him found soothing. It created the illusion of escape into other worlds, of dim cafés and lovers, of love, physical contact and sensuous pleasures, an illusion which flees the light of day. Its words are about a promised land, about love gained and love lost.

The record turned a cat's purr noise, a hum that slowly brought it to a close. His eyes were closed. The closing of eyes that were tired but never knew that they were tired till you closed them. She moved and sat on the arm of the chair. He instinctively reached for her with his right arm and held her in a half embrace, as the song talked of the promised land and love.

Suddenly she got up. Then he heard the clinking of glasses, and a drink was being poured. If he had opened his eyes, he would have seen it. But he saw it even in the darkness of his closed eyes. The tall glass on which was drawn a black chef with his cap, grinning. The smell of beer, foaming with a hiss to the brim.

Here.

He stretched out his hand and grabbed it. Eyes still closed. He lifted it up to his lips and took a pull. A long pull of bittersweet hops and malt foaming into his moustache. The liquid coursed down his throat burning cold. He held up the pull to take a breath, and pulled again.

As he was handing the glass to her he opened his eyes. He was at peace. He breathed a long breath and took another look at her. Outside the cars were passing with screeches on the corner curb. The street voices sounded distant and faint. He was at peace.

Do you want to eat now?

Yes.

She moved over to the big table. He kept his eyes on her. She opened a pan, inspected its contents and placed it on the table. She pulled out another pan, bigger than the first, peered inside and placed that too near the first. She bent down and from under the bed pulled a hot plate stove, wires dangling. She placed the hot plate on the big table, plugged the wire, and waited. Then she placed the first pan on the reddening plate. She picked from a cardboard box underneath the table a big spoon. Soon the steam from the pan began to rise; she stirred the contents gently. She moved away and sat on the bed, and looked at the food simmering. Its smell had by now taken possession of the whole room.

He was holding the glass newly filled with beer, now and then taking a sip and looking at her. The smile had gone. But the look of contentment which the beer and the music produced was still there on his face.

She rose up. She walked up to the table. She stirred the food once more, and lifted it up from the hot plate. She picked up the second pan and placed it on the red coils. From underneath, in the cardboard box, she collected two enamel plates, green with a red band. She wiped them with a white napkin hanging on the line over the bed. She brought out two forks and two spoons. She carried them to the round table on which his legs were resting. She dished out the food, gauging with her eyes the quantity he ate. He usually ate very little. Most of the time. At times he would indulge a little and ask for more. But that was rare.

They sat now facing each other not saying a word. There was always a time to speak and a time to refrain from speaking. They ate in silence. The silence of love, of the communion of two people who shared more beyond the passion of words. She ate slowly, picking her food like a bird, elegantly, and swallowing the morsels with quiet relish. He ate, a little noisily at first, but after a few sizable morsels he ate noiselessly now, and his eyes wanted more beer. His this night was the contented happiness of inner peace.

When they finished eating, he drank another glass of beer which she had poured. He put his head back on the cushion, and began to read his and her life on the white ceiling marked by rain water burrowed lines running like a serpent from one corner to another. Its head, placed below the wooden beam that held the ceiling together, asleep. When he saw this mark the first time some months ago, he was startled even though he knew it wasn't a snake. The awareness of the serpent overhead stayed with him always, whenever he came, whenever he slept on the bed, whenever he kissed her, whenever he got ready to leave in the dead of night.

He looked at it closely now. Its brown colour had been deepened by more rain water of late, and it was becoming heavier in the middle as if it had swallowed a creature. It was even beginning to grow feet like a centipede.

Adisa had one day quarrelled with the landlord, a drunken pensioner who lived next door and sang the same song every day after meals, when he came to collect his rent. It was over the leaking roof, but more over the serpent. The man looked at her, smiled, pocketed the money, and said, Menya wo aye, and walked away.

She went to the bed and began to remove the clothes on it. She folded them and packed them on the big table. Then she made the bed, smoothed all the folds in the sheet, and replaced the foot cloth after shaking it. She went back to the arm of the chair. He held her with his right hand again in the same silent embrace.

He got up and began to undress. First he took off his trousers. His shirt hung loosely over his underpants. He loosened his collar, first by the studs, and unfastened the cuff links. Then he removed the shirt over his head. It was an old habit from schooldays when as a boy he wore shirts that were removed only over the head because they had no front buttons. He folded the shirt and placed it on the arm of the second chair. He bent down and took off his socks. They smelled a bit.

Meanwhile she had moved up to the door and closed it gently. She turned the Yale knob inside to lock it. She slowly, in front of the dressing mirror, removed her loincloth. She was wearing a pink pantie underneath. Her breasts, released now from the grip of the cloth, came to life, erect. The nipples were thick, and blacker than the rest of the breast. She looked at herself in the mirror. She smiled to her shadow in the mirror. She turned round and moved towards the bed.

He was reclining on the edge of the bed, his hands beneath his head, looking at the serpent. She moved first with her right leg across him and then her left leg. She eased her body on to the bed slowly. She turned to him. He turned to her away from the serpent, away from the world away from everything.

Slowly she removed his underwear. This was her ritual. She did it because she loved to hold him in the midriff as she removed his underwear. Then she slid out of hers. He was hot and ready, blazing like a thousand fires in a parched forest land. With his left forefinger he drew a line like the serpent down her body into her pubic hair which was hard and shiny – she played gently with the hair on his chest. She drew near. He drew nearer.

And they were lost in the mist of their singular soul. His movement was gentle slow deliberate. Hers was quick. She was crying. Soft low moans. He realized that a thin line of water was running down the side of his left eye. He was crying too. Their dreams asleep and awake were one. This was the hour of their redemption washed clean by tears brewed from the anguish of the singular soul.

## ••• *Chapter 4a*

The smell of coital semen in the dry heat of a little room restores the shattered nerves jangled in a neat bundle upon a bed.

My cousin Dede she was born of my aunt who died in her birth my first love in the fields of wild flowers and butterflies long long ago she came from the dead in the shape of the woman of the sea, emerged where the moon slashed the sea in two with her burning sword years years ago under the Indian almond tree. She led me through the grass plains of our infancy through the shower days through my birch tree and pinewood summers in Middlesex to the shores of Tun Hu in China across the vastness of the dream lands of Soviet Russia the canefields of Oriente Province in Cuba to the hills the hills of Mexico – pronounced Mehico by the natives – along neat out-of-town farms on the one forty-five to Oxford to see Neville with Kodzo chatting slowly to the hum of the train about the revolution.

Then she died. Then she returned, my woman of the sea with black nipples a tooth extracted by the dentist who squeezed her breast and she bit his hand in the guise of the tall ochre-skinned girl comely and cannot read or write who sat every day when I came home on holiday facing our house selling bread. We never spoke a word. But we knew we had signed a pact with our eyes. Then I searched for my friend Agbavor he was in Standard Five then, I had gone on to college, and he gave us his room. I went over across the street and told her. She agreed. She only nodded her head. That evening when the evening angelus rang she came carrying a knitted tablecloth on which was written in myriad coloured threads, 'I love you my darlling' spelled with double *l*. Much as I tried on the reed mat with a pillow I could not find her. She was also green, and struggled. Then in the shame of sixteen years I arose and went away my knees all bruised. I hid around the gate hatching a story to tell should father ask, What happened to your knees? Then I'll say, I fell down from the sheep eye tree outside our house this afternoon. But no one ever asked. And the wound, young wound, healed quick. I went back to school and told a tall tale to my friends about my conquest. They believed it for they wanted to believe what did not happen to them.

Then the other one her head flat like a tadpole's, with a slow gentle gait like a royal python. With her I spoke words remembered from Nomalizo, wrote her words remembered from the Presbyterian hymnbook about you my only star on whom I fix my gaze the strong stone on whom I lean my food my drink my pillow and everything to me. She replied and quoted the third stanza of the same hymn as I had quoted the first. I never saw her again.

The years rolled precariously through pubic growth to the first real itches unwarrantable and fictitious as witches. Then I came home one vacation. She was a slim wet-lipped girl with large buttocks and swinging hips who hawked ground nuts straight into bachelors' bedrooms. When she came into mine I didn't ask any questions. She left laughing down the stairway into the night. She agreed out of sheer benevolence and a sense of charity written large upon her like her headkerchief. She came again. And each time was a different journey into the open mysteries of life's incarnation.

Then followed wild years with Irish tarts in Brixton. There was one with the face like a lost crocodile who talked about love and marriage and a journey back home to Africa over the ocean when we will make love and create half-caste children – veritable bats of our homecoming. But I got tired of her wateriness and fled to North London. There was a thin ghostlike one with distant eyes redolent of misty winters who insisted on coming home with me after a wild party in Chelsea and froze in my arms in my bed. She confessed she went with other women. The bitch. I never saw her again.

The long summers melted into autumns and winters of intense loneliness as I dreamed of the school latrine at home where a banana grove bushes throughout the year where as little devilish boys we asked Wosikpo to take off her dress so that we could inspect her baby hole. One boy tried to put his forefinger into it and she screamed that she was going to tell her mother. So we fled. Now the train has come and I must go to Wembley Park. The Bakerloo line goes to Wembley Park, doesn't it? The question is surprising for there is a route map right above her. Yes, I said, you dumb thing. We rode, silent.

Where are you from? Ghana. Isn't that the Gold Coast? Yes, before independence, before emancipation. The train rolled along through Swiss Cottage, Kilburn, Willesden Green, Dollis Hill to Wembley Park. I stuck my books under my arms. A word was not spoken after the preliminary proddings. She was a tall-legged girl scarcely nineteen with teeth like corals and a smile like an instant spring in the middle of winter. She walked after me. We presented our tickets. Did I know where such and such a road was? Yes. We walked, our footfalls ringing on the pavement as cars sped past us full of laughing youth hell bound. I reached my street. Won't you come in for a cup of tea? Yes, I will. My room was in a mess, law journals scattered everywhere, notes on pieces of paper copied from expensive books glanced at in the library at the Inn. Soon the kettle was whistling like a nearby Boy Scout jamboree in session. We drank three cups each. She took off her clothes slowly and lay on my bed. She stayed for two weeks till my landlady, the Jewish woman who hated Israel and Jews, came and drove her off.

Loving the memory of her my first love through all lands and all climes, searching for her who came out of the sea in the shadow of the almond tree whilst they searched for me with lanterns. We walked the lanes, I remember, and lay in the shadow of the church Christmas Eve when they sang 'While Shepherds Watched Their Flocks by Night', we lay in the sand as the sea at home hummed, hummed a hymn of lost travellers and the three wise men and three blind mice see how they run.

Wash my feet with the perfumes you bought on that trip to Lome when we stayed at Hotel de Gulf and made plans and cried for each other, for the malevolent knowledge that I must go away tormented you. I burned seven incenses for you at the high altar of my church and showed you to my uncle.

Tall, she sat her eyes dreaming and staring at my naked soul. She came home and we fell in love very romantically, fell hopelessly in love. We kept it going, stoking a lot of emotional fuel into the furnace to keep it ablaze aburning. Then she became pregnant. I was not ready for marriage. We found somebody who came and gave her things and stuck a machine into her vagina and the baby was killed. Two weeks after scarcely the wound had healed we fell upon each other in our sorrow. Then we made more plans. Then friends came and said they saw her with other men. Her denial was firm and adamant. But we knew it was over. After a brief quarrel she stormed out and soon became pregnant for another man. She now has two children, by my last count, according to the rumours.

Her father called me to a meeting with my father about the ways of his daughter with me. My father swore his son was a perfect son who did not know a woman. He should go and put reins upon his daughter who was a young whore at seventeen. Years after I met her. She is grown very fat and married to an innocent-looking man with a sad dog face.

I found her among the dancers sweating on the floor in one of those wild new dances of youth. She is my woman of the sea. She is the one who appeared through the cleft sea in the slash of the moonbeam to come to me under the Indian almond. She led me then through all farmlands, she led me over the wide lagoon where the sprats sang a song from the salt basins, over bird island we flew with the gulls returning from sea, over the sugar cane farms over the lagoon landing stage into the strange land, into Lave the forest of animals where we sat under my grandfather's blackberry tree as my uncle came with a smoked duiker caught in his trap as his dog Katsekpo jumped jumped like the District Commissioner's dog in the grass. She laughed revealing where the dentist removed her tooth while we chattered with the weaver birds overhead about old matters in bootlike nests in the market place.

My stones and oil lamps wore rings of rainbows, and shadows run like the ghosts of my beginning, whining nims of May in the storm of sowing season's rains into the fire-exit of the future exile. For love's passion flees to the moon slanted in a pee pose her legs long astride the ocean where her sword blazed that day in the urinal hour to find me under the Indian almond.

Dear one, hold on, for I come.

## ••• *Chapter 5*

The church festivals of the school were important events in the lives of every schoolboy. The children worked hard towards Easter, Christmas and Children's Day. Easter demanded two attendances at church service, and communicants went to confession the previous day to prepare to eat the body and drink the blood of Our Lord. Easter hymns were relearned and dark cloths got ready for Good Friday.

The elders always frowned on the women singing at dawn. It outraged the gods, they said. And the gods of the land were abroad at dawn. This could bring famine, smallpox and leprosy upon the people. Kakabiku got drunk and abused the church leaders in song. His song said if a man called Yesu Kristo was beaten and crucified in Jerusalem many many years ago what had it to do with you, Papa Timotheo. Your daughter is a prostitute in Accra, go and bring her home. Kakabiku said if he were there when they were beating him he would say, Beat him hard. But he would rise up again, he would come out of his grave. Who had died and come out before?

Good Friday was a day the children enjoyed. That was the day they clubbed their own Judas Iscariot made with old clothes. They made merry. They called on friends, and raided palm wine groves. They escaped their mothers' vigilance to go to the palm wine groves. They brought home bubbling morning palm wine. And got drunk in the afternoon when the wine turned sour. Their stomachs ran and they defecated on the compound and got shamed for it.

It was unheard of for a boy to miss church service. Any boy who didn't attend was asking for his transfer certificate.

Paku didn't come to Palm Service and Good Friday because of his animal traps. They were his only source of income. From them he got money to buy his school uniforms, pay his fees, give himself morning coppers, and buy his books. He was older than most of the boys. Rumour had it that he had a wife tucked away in his mother's village in Kave. He went to see about his animal traps at Easter. So he missed the route march into town with palm branches and the two services.

Monday morning. The school assembled. A long list of boys who 'dodged' these serious events was announced. If you didn't come to both events you got twelve lashes; if you missed one, six. The teachers stood on the edges of the assembly smiling, their eyes flashing, waiting to be the dispensers of God's wrath on religious defaulters. A few of the boys were caned and they hobbled into their places rubbing their buttocks with both hands.

Paku was the next.

I won't take it, he said, his eyes red with quiet anger.

What did you say?

I say I won't take the lashes! This time he shouted defiantly at the Headmaster, who stood speechless staring at him. It was unheard of. Discipline had broken down in his school. Unheard of.

Mr Adama, bring class Four register. There and then, Paku's name was crossed out with red ink. This was to be a lesson to all boys. Disobedient boys had no place in Deme Roman Catholic School so long as he remained Headmaster.

Paku walked into class Four classroom, pulled down every cupboard and picked out his exercise books. Arithmetic, Dictation, Civics, Nature Study, English, Vernacular, Hygiene and Religious Knowledge. He walked out to the compound, the envy and alarm of every boy.

Two terms after he appeared at the school. In army uniform. The little boys followed him all through town. He had a jackknife dangling from his side. And he smoked a cigarette! He shook hands with all the teachers including the Headmaster, who was then teaching class Five. The Headmaster delivered a little speech and said everyone should brighten the corner where he was. Was it not the stone which the builders rejected which became the head of the corner?

After the black mournful atmosphere of Good Friday on which the son of God was crucified, to save all from sin, everyone settled down and awaited the Resurrection.

Easter Sunday broke at 3 a.m., that is, at the first cock. Easter songs woke you up from afar. It was a dream.

In vain they sealed the tomb,
He arose, he arose.
Hallelujah, Christ arose!

The women sang and the handbells beat time and you would dream you were with the angels in heaven and they were singing. The resurrected Christ sat on a golden stool covered with a huge blue cloth taken down from the entrance of the medicine hut where the brekete drums were silent. The angels were wearing white calico walking the lanes of God's town. They were ringing a handbell to beat time.

He arose, he arose.
Hallelujah, Christ arose!

The voices drifted farther and farther away and came back to wake you up because they had stopped, to begin a new tune, and to beat time with the handbells. Now and then the voices of the women became the voices of angels in white sheets encircling the golden stool.

He is the King and he the Captain,
Victor in the hard-won fight,
God of life and resurrection.

People said that the women wore bed sheets, but the Christian women whether in bed sheets or not rejoiced at Resurrection in the knowledge that the final sacrament of their Lord saved them all from sin. Christ arose for Deme too, and earth and heaven prolonged the strain of the joyful tidings.

The service started at nine-thirty; white cloth and the smell of talcum.

So, Lord, to those who sleep in thee
Shall new and glorious bodies be.

The great war 1939–1945. The great Empire was at war with Nazi Germany, and England expected everyone to do his duty.

Orders came from the District Commissioner that the schools must make a 'war effort' to help the Allies who were fighting to preserve the Empire. They must collect palm kernels, shell them, and send the nuts to England. They must collect pennies to help starving children who were orphaned and some crippled by the bombs of Nazi Germany.

New songs came. About the war. The most popular was

Hitler is trying hard,
Trying hard to take Togoland,
Gold Coast, Nigeria,
Sierra Leone and Gambia
And make them his own.
Chorus: Oh, Hitler, your nose is big,
Your penis is crooked.

Airplanes came and dropped leaflets with pictures of Winston Churchill, a big cigar in his mouth. Slogans were also dropped, 'Buy British Bombers to Bomb Berlin', 'We Will Win', 'V for Victory'. Then you made the sign at passing cars and army convoys that were lost in the dust of the road when the rains had gone.

The mobile cinema vans came regularly. They showed films of smart British soldiers marching to martial music and queueing for hot steaming food grinning from ear to ear. That was war. Quick montages of battle action, smoke and confusion. And a few British soldiers would be leading towards camera a long line of captive Germans.

Then the vans came to let people 'sign their names' to go and join in this glorious carnage of conquest in the name of the Empire. There were opportunities to learn trades. Young men were shown drilling with guns, driving smart jeeps, carpentering, learning to manoeuvre big ponderous machines in huge forbidding buildings.

Many young men enlisted. Some escaped home after a few weeks swearing by their grandfathers' coffins that they would never be soldiers. A few weeks after they were hunted down by the police. There were midnight stampedes of running feet, blowing of whistles and swinging torchlights when a deserter was tracked down to a house. A few vanished into the bush, shaved their heads, and became herbalists and native doctors.

But not all deserted. Among the band of young men who left Deme was Yawo Letsu, one of the leading drummers of the town. He joined the queue one morning in the market place while the music blared from the van. His heart beat fast. He was defying his father. Stories of the war reached him. He would not have wanted to join if it wasn't for Avonyo, a member of his age group, a farmer like himself. Avonyo had joined one morning and had vanished. A few months later he appeared in army uniform, boots so shiny you could really see your face in them, and a jackknife. He said he was on leave. After a gay two weeks during which he slept with the best girls in town, bought drinks for everyone, and gave his mother a fortune of ten shillings he vanished again. Yawo decided firmly. Either a soldier or nothing. He would not spend his life here bruising his palms every sowing season, hitting a succession of deerskins wrapped around hollowed tree trunks called drums.

Rumours had it people were being killed. They mentioned Adzowa Sesime's son who was always in Accra and became a soldier. They said he died in Burma. But no one confirmed this piece of news. But a man was born to die.

The voice of the enlisting sergeant, an N.T. man with a small face and sharp red eyes, split his ears.

Next! What be your name?

Yawo Letsu.

Wen dey born you?

Yawo didn't understand the second question. He turned round to the interpreter, who said, Gbekagbe wodzi wo?

Nye me nya o.

He doesn't know.

You must put sah every time you hamser ques. O.K.?

Yes sah.

He say e don't know when dey born am.

Yes sah.

What age e get?

About twenty-five, sah.
You be im father?
No sah.
But how you know?
I sabe him mother.
E get any sickness?
Ebe dolelea de le nuwoa?
Ao.
No sah.
E no get sickness from woman?
Elo nue kpoa.
Ao.
What be im father name?
Kwasi Letsu.
Ibe farmer.
Do kae wo wo na.
Agbledo.
Next!

Komi Gale was next. He was a bright-eyed lad who had been apprenticed as a carpenter. He hated the work. He escaped from the carpentry shed this morning to come and enlist. The recruiting sergeant looked at him from head to foot.

Attention!

Komi brought his feet together. The sergeant circled him, looked at his feet and shook his head.

Your foot ino gree.

His left foot was slightly larger than the right one. It was gnarled by guinea worm when he was a boy.

Next!

Komi still stood, looking expectantly at the sergeant.

Wobe woafo medzo o. Wo me tenu xowo ge o.

He couldn't believe his ears. His feet. His left foot. But they were not going to fight with feet! No. He must go to soldier. He begged the big man.

Shurrup! Next.

Komi withdrew from the line. He paced slowly towards the carpentry shed. His mates had almost finished the chair they all had started yesterday.

What is the matter? They didn't take you?

No. It is my left foot.

We told you they wouldn't take you.

But why; I don't understand.

They can't get boots to fit you.

He fell silent, and mused the whole day. A plan slowly formed in his head. He would go to Accra and enlist. Accra was the place.

Most of the boys were enlisted. Some of the best drummers and young farmers, the props of their families. They went away leaving behind young wives and suckling babies to fight in the white man's war.

The sergeant made a brief speech.

Men, they go take you for Amkra for Teshie camp. There you go make emseisais, learn for how dem soot for gun; go learn what them call tactic. When ifinis learn ebriting, whewm! You go for Hisa Africa. Sometiem from Hisa Africa you go go for Burma self I no know; that one day for the hand of beturi. O.K. All correct! Jamp himsad for truck and make we go.

A great shout greeted this speech after it was translated. The men scrambled for places in the truck. Wives and mothers and old women cried, some wailed, a few wept silently. An old woman was whimpering near the roadside, her crying turned into a song, a dirge for the dead.

I tell you, do not go; stay and tend the farm, stay and feed me till I die. Ao, Ao, Ao, an animal has caught me. A snake has bitten me, to whom shall I tell it, to whom shall I tell?

Her last remaining son, Bawa, had enlisted.

The sergeant had said anyone who withdrew or left the truck would be regarded as a deserter. The law of the army would deal with him proper proper. Some missed a heartbeat, but all was well. The sergeant was sharp, confident, a soldier. His clothes were neat, his boots shone, and he had a jackknife. There was nothing to fear.

Sergeant Mama Seidu came from the north. He belonged to the Dagomba tribe. He came south when he was thirteen to find work because the land was infertile. Life was becoming hard for his aging father's family of five wives and eighteen children. He was the third child of the first wife. Rumour came up north announcing good work. Work with white men. Lads came back now and then in trousers and shoes and shirts. One or two even brought home bicycles. Mama left his village with ten shillings saved from selling wild guinea fowls he had trapped. He walked two days to Tamale where he boarded a southbound mammy truck for Kumasi. His money got finished, and after two days when he lived on kola nuts, he found a job as a houseboy for a white man who worked at the P.W.D. He prospered on three pounds a month. When the war broke out, his master, who loved the R.A.F. and talked of his days as pilot-officer, took the boat to join his countrymen. Before leaving he paid Mama a handsome pension of twenty pounds. He persuaded him to join the army. Mama joined. And had not regretted it. He could not go on active service because his left leg was shorter than the right, a mishap that occurred in his boyhood days when he walked into an antelope trap. He limped slightly since then. He rose fast because he was sharp, efficient and clever. The pay was good. He was liked by his superiors. He got his three ropes in just under two years. His recruiting work, assisted by a corporal who wrote and read, was exhilarating. That was his war.

Yawo Letsu's father came near the truck. He wanted to speak to his son. The sergeant walked round to where he stood. He warned him that, if he didn't want trouble with government and beturi in Amkra, he should remove himself and his smelly pipe. Kwasi Letsu left, his heart heavy with grief. He offered his son to the gods, to the ancestors.

The truck took off amidst cheers, tears and wailing. It gathered speed near the big Ago palm and vanished beyond the village in a thick cloud of dust.

Some died in Burma. A few returned home to kill their wives for sleeping with other men and for spending their allotment. One in particular cut his uncle in the stomach while he was eating bean cakes with a matchet for squandering the money government paid him for being a soldier. Some came home mad. Among them was Abotsi.

The children knew him very well. He used to come and sit on the compound, and sometimes do odd jobs. He was gentle. He wasn't actually mad. He was eccentric. He would salvage from the dunghill dead goats and fowls.

He would come and sit quietly under the coconut tree on the compound. And tell stories of his days in Burma. He was a magazine carrier. He said, The Japanese are good fighters.

They are short with eyes near their ears, and as quick as bamboo squirrels. We captured one one day sleeping in a bamboo grove. We were marching him to camp. Suddenly he jumped up with a yell and started running. The sergeant said Stop! No. He ran fast. Somebody fired at him. It was me. Yes, it was me who fired. I was very brave. He fell down. He was bleeding. He had been hit in the leg. We brought him to camp. On the way he spoke Japanese. We had double ration that day. And the officer, his name was, now what was his name? Poker, that was his name.

He would ramble on and on about rations, Japanese, ghosts, guns, deaths, wounds, everything.

He had the habit of attending dances. He would stand at the edge of the dance hall, his eyes on the drinks on the tables. The owners of the drinks had gone to dance. Then like a hawk he would swoop down on the tables and gulp down the drink in every glass and withdraw. When they caught him and questioned him, he would deny and challenge those who had caught him to smell his breath. No one was keen on smelling Abotsi's breath. So he got away. They said he was involved in a fight with the caretaker of the Zion Mission Compound because he had jumped over a wall and sneaked into a cantata show by a choir from Lome. If you asked him what happened before his forehead became as huge as Adaklu hillock, he would look angry.

You children don't respect your elders.

He would be coaxed with a plate of beans. He would sit down and eat. At intervals he would let off a grunt and say, People don't know.

When he finished his food, he would ask, Do you know what happened to my forehead?

After a brief silence he would give an answer. I fell down near the wall in front of Pandora house.

Abotsi, you are lying, you were beaten by Topa!

Tsia! He can't beat me. It was I who beat him.

So the secret would be out. You daren't tease him if he was hungry. It was dangerous.

After his discharge in 1946, he took part in the Victory Parade. He didn't know where his service uniforms were.

They said when he came home from Burma, he did not perform the purification ceremony which was required. So the ghosts of the Japanese he killed followed him. And made him mad. He did not perform the ceremony because he did not have money. It was expensive. Anything he saved he spent on his food. He spent market days at the lorry park doing 'booker' work, loading and unloading mammy trucks. He was very popular with the lorry drivers and the women.

One evening during the harmattan season, a few days to Christmas, he came to the house wrapped in his only khaki coat looking very subdued. He was either hungry or angry or both. A plate of sprat soup and akple was pushed towards him. He looked at it and shook his head.

Abotsi, won't you eat? Eat!

He first sat there and shook his head.

Go and call tailor, children.

Tailor was the only one who could deal with Abotsi. They were fast friends even though they would quarrel over silly matters. Tailor fought anyone who tried to cheat Abotsi.

He came and stood near him. He knew his friend very well.

Hoso, hoso, man pass man, position pass power. The funeral gun you are not a hunter, a hunter is different. What is the matter?

Abotsi always replied to rum names and such brave salutations – when his stomach was full – with a long hearty laugh. Today he was silent, staring at the well in the centre of the compound.

Abotsi, what is the matter with you? Come on, don't sit here behaving like a silly woman. What is the matter?

Abotsi, pricked by the degrading comparison, turned round and pointed to his stomach.

What is the matter with your stomach?

He was mute. Suddenly he bent down, clutching his stomach.

Our mother, do you have any medicine?

A bottle of concocted herb was produced. He gulped down a spoonful and made faces. The children laughed.

His stomach had been running.

Is it gone?

Hm.

What did you eat today? You ate a dead fowl?

He didn't answer. He sat propped against the coconut tree, and stared at the well.

Suddenly he threw himself down groaning.

I will die, I will die.

He rolled on the ground as far as the well.

Tailor came rushing in. He was middle-aged, and as he himself said, had been rich once upon a time. He had worked with the famous District Commissioner, John Miller, to build the road from Keta to the Volta River and beyond. He had been strong once. After that he made money smuggling akpeteshie, the local gin which the colonial government declared unwholesome. One day a lorry carrying a large quantity of his gin was arrested at the riverside. The drink was poured into the river; he himself was arrested at Fiaxo where he had taken refuge. After two years in prison he came back home, broken. His three wives had married other people, three of his sons had gone up country into the cocoa area, the other two had joined a fishing company in Abidjan. His daugher Amavi took the mammy truck and vanished to Accra. She had not been home since. Tailor fell back on the old trade he had half learned as a young man, hired a sewing machine and mended clothes. He had no orders for new clothes. No one trusted his expertise. Nobody gave him credit and whenever he told the story of his past, he would shake his head and say, The hands that have eaten with chiefs and now become like this! It is difficult, it is difficult for a camel to pass through the needle of an eye.

One day he chased the catechist from the Methodist Church with a matchet because he came to collect church dues.

Thieves and liars! Was I the one they saw before they built their church? Let him come here again asking for money.

They say if you don't pay your dues, you won't be given Christian burial, someone would say.

My father and his father before him were not given Christian burial. Are they not at rest? Sons of prostitutes, if I die and they don't bury me I won't care a foolish nonsense. I am dead and gone. Rubbish. They collect money and share among themselves, the thieves! Let him come here again and I will let him see the contents of his stomach.

One day, they whispered that he was dying. He had been drinking the previous day and had not eaten. People came to see the dying man. He lay on his bed, his lantern glowing lowly. He was breathing hard.

I am dying. Is there anyone with a pencil and paper?

Someone had.

Write down the names I am going to call. They owe me money. Collect the money. Use it to buy a coffin for me.

A few elders had gathered looking at him. They were sure he was dying. There was nothing they could do.

Before I close my mouth, Gamadeku, go and tell your wife to cook me akple and some light soup. I can't die on empty stomach.

The food was brought. He ate and burst into a big sweat. He didn't die. The next day he was about abusing one of his creditors near the fig tree.

He and Abotsi had struck up a strange friendship over the years. The friendship of equals. He protected him, abused people for him and was prepared to fight his battles at any time. Both fought each other now and then.

He bent over Abotsi and touched his head. I think he has fever too. What shall we do?

Let's take him to hospital.

Someone rushed out and hailed a taxi. They carried him out of the compound into the street. When the taxi driver saw him he yelled and called him his rum name.

So this is my passenger. The world is changing. He opened the rear door and added that Abotsi was pretending. Has he eaten?

No.

Then why are you worried? He is only hungry.

You take us to the hospital and stop your rubbish mouth. Tailor was getting angry.

At the hospital, they carried him into one of the wards. A male nurse rushed in. Take him out, take him out at once.

Why? tailor asked.

They took him out and put him on the veranda. Tailor went to the chief nurse and told what happened. Could the doctor come and see him?

Doctor! What! You don't mean we should phone doctor because Abotsi is ill? What!

Please, we beg you, please.

He looked up briefly and rolled towards a telephone. He was fat and exuded extra food snatched from patients too ill to eat.

Is that doctor? . . . Yes sir; no sir; I know him.

No, he is not exactly mad. No sir.

All right, sir. Tomorrow then, sir.

A nurse came and stood near. She looked round at the people, at the patient, and turned away muttering something about people who smelled like he-goats being brought into hospitals.

How we are suffering, she said, walking away, wriggling her hips.

Doctor can't come. Bring him tomorrow.

Please, sir, help.

I say bring him tomorrow; can't you hear?

That night Abotsi died in tailor's room. Tailor came and said it in whispers at early dawn. They didn't want the children to hear.

What can we do?

Can they agree to bury him?

I will try.

Tailor came back at early morning, the sun was just rising over the Methodist Church.

They say they can't. He was not a member. What can we do?

Try the Presbyterians.

Tailor came back about ten dripping sweat.

They say they can't – he is not baptized.

What can we do?

A deep silence hung around the house.

We must bury him today.

There is a pagan cemetery. I will try. He came back about three. I have got a place for him.

That afternoon, a small procession left tailor's house. All the bookers from the lorry park had come. The coffin was cheap. Four of his friends carried it. Then Beneza opened his hymnbook and called the words of the hymns from memory. The procession moved slowly from Princess Street through Market Road, and took the turn near the Lome station on to Fort Road into Akpa's coconut trees and past the cinema house.

Shall I sorrow in life's need?
I do not covet even a crown here.
Here they nailed my Saviour to a tree
And they put a crown of thorns upon his head.

No one cried. The children from the house followed at a distance. Their mother had forbidden them to come. But they knew him. Especially the wild-eyed strapping lad of twelve. He was his friend. He gave him snail tops and trimmed them for him.

When the procession reached the cemetery, it had to wait because the diggers had not finished making the grave. Beneza performed the service. Every death was his.

Now the labourer's task is over.

Three, four!

Then the shovels pushed the mounds of earth on to the cheap coffin. They left one by one. Smoking their crumpled tuskers. That night there was a wake. The agbadza boys brought their drums. There were two tins of akpeteshie. They drummed and sang till the third cock.

The wild-eyed lad slept fitfully that night. He saw him in his dreams, sitting propped against the coconut tree staring at the well, telling long tales of Burma and Japanese and rations, and of magic over guns.

# ••• *Chapter 5a*

Hitler had only one ball. That was the song. Floated through our mornings and noons in palm groves as mobile cinema vans came and Gold Coast film units came and shot films of kernel gatherers. Elders asked, When are you coming back to show it to us, we want to take copies, I will take five copies. Stories of death in bamboo groves when they crossed the Kalapanzi River when he fought in the 81st Division South East Asia Command mentioned in two dispatches; one for gallantry and one for – he'd forgotten the second one. They slept with white women, Burmese women, in riverside huts or in the slum section of Rangoon, on the boat home they stopped off Alexandria and raided the town in black convoys and Christ died on the cross.

He arose again on the third day.
He is not here! For he is risen as he said.

Convoys float through dust-covered haze for days on end grim rattling on gravel roads towards where no one knows. East Africa, Tanganyika, Burma, India – Royal West Africa Frontier Force. Death stalked in ambush in distant lands propitiations and magic potions prepared here cannot cross oceans as the white man's gun does not understand the language of black magic.

Bend down, the tall boys at the back come forward, put them on your backs you will receive twelve lashes each and then you will learn not to miss the holy feasts of the Church through Jesus Christ our Lord, Amen.

Qui seminant in lacrimis, in gaudio metent,

and the holy martyrs of the Holy Catholic Church with our Papa in Roma has sent the holy order that all shall obey the laws of the Church, follow the directions of their bishops in these turbulent days of war, and prayer and supplication must continue in these terrible days and to the guidance of Christ I commend you all the Holy Father. The troops that went to Abyssinia received his holy blessings too. We were nourished by the sacrament of salvation, by the booming voice of Father James and Bishop Herman the Blessed we believe he will be canonized in God's own time in Roma for he died in the Lord's vineyard in the service of the Holy Catholic Church in Lome.

> Nor consider that it is expedient for us, that
> one man should die for the people, and that the
> whole nation perish not.
>
> St John

Kayi wawa, beturi kayi wawa, sadzi medzo kayi wawa na bongo ee kayi wawa, kayi wawa beturi.

Those feet tramped through the jungles of Burma for King and country, and Empire.

To be true and worthy members of the Empire, we must maintain unshaken our faith in God, in the Empire and in ourselves. God bless you all.

On the path of dust to palm groves where tappers' feet had fashioned a way in the sand held firm by elephant grass was a long army of driver ants. Their road led to the red earth hillock smaller by far than the hillock of Calvary.

My brother and I we played games as hunters with our catapult in a bamboo grove among a massed gang of squirrels screaming squeaky insults as our missiles of hand-baked shiny clay slashed through bamboo leaves and puffed-up tails of squirrels changed position in mid-air. We killed a few. We held a feast outside, with pepper, onions, tomatoes – we raided old man Timotheo's orchard for the last item, ran as he chased us in a blind fury, blind as a bat, through a hole in the fence made by stray goats belonging to Kwasivi, the man who owned the ground tank beside our house. He lost an arm years after and died. So Father said. Squirrel meat on salt, pepper and tomatoes is a feast for gods. From there, my brother, the greedy pig, went and ate dzemkple and eggs just having been offered to a wayside god in Ablome; he came home his mouth oozing palm oil. What did you eat? Sacrifice. What? It is evil. You will die. I won't. It looked too good to let alone. And dogs would eat it if I didn't. But we just ate a meal of squirrels. You will die, I said. He didn't die, not then. Years, twenty-five years after, of typhoid that killed him in three days. The church was insistent that he was not baptized. Father, angry and erect, cursed them soundly when his baptismal date was found in an old parish register spelled in the crawling calligraphy of a priest long long dead. At his wake, we sat and watched the agbadza boys drum the whole night and my cousin Victor played hymns on his whining accordion to send my brother's soul to heaven, as Father sat sad-eyed. I went with a few of the boys from Accra, as we sat into the morning dew and intoned

Mawu, Mawu, le Kristo fe vu ta
Na wom be ku malilim o

to the background of agbadza drums and the raising of dust by naked feet on Father's compound. We laid plans which of the girls at the wake would make good mates for the remainder of the night. I ended with a tall giantess with the dazzling beauty of a gazelle possessed of insatiable capacity to love all night. She brought a meal the next day as my uncle sat in the parlour of the resthouse drunk as a chief – he is a chief – and passed lewd comments on my night lover's anatomic details with an embarrassing accuracy. Months after I went back to see her. Her husband had come down from somewhere in Ashanti. I met him, shook hands with him, fled gently into the dark night near the acacia tree.

So, Lord, to those who sleep in thee
Shall new and glorious bodies be.

Some came home mad from Burma; Dzesan ran amok one gay sunny market day, shouldered a musket and opened fire on the market of screaming women and children. It took three medicine men and ten police constables to overcome him. They led him away boasting about the number of Japanese he had killed and the government had cheated him out of his money. There was another, Sule. He put himself in uniform, made one for his five-year-old son, and marched with the infant from dawn till noon every market day on the main road singing 'Kayiwawa beturi', the theme song of his Burmese days. He screamed orders at his platoon – i.e., his five-year-old son – who responded in little jerks, sweat streaming down his comely little face. His Father's eyes would be red as he screamed. Halt, rendebaure, tien, elem, ra, elem, ra, and marched into the opposite end towards Lome station his jackknife dangling.

The day we came to chapel the Headmaster said Hitler was dead, we screamed a wild joy and went on holidays. Our enemy who wanted to enslave us was dead. We the loyal subjects of the King screamed with joy when our enemy died.

On Victory Day, the soldiers marched in never ending columns at Moganu – some didn't have uniforms; they were rumoured to have sold them to farmers – an impressive array of men, giants, their faces glistening in the morning sun. The District Commissioner read an address and the men marched weary till sundown. There was a great booze-up that day, all over town. We followed some of them we knew who had run away from school to Burma.

Years, later, twenty-five years later, my brother died of typhoid fever.

A man was caught for stealing turkey. As the crowd yelled and the turkey owner slapped him loudly he kept on screaming, I don't eat animals of blood, I eat fish. They led him towards the police station in the dying twilight screaming, I don't eat animals of blood, I eat fish.

## ••• *Chapter 6*

It was already two-thirty. He lifted up his head and looked at the clock on the big table. He looked at his wristwatch. It also said two-thirty.

She was sleeping on her side, gently snoring. She would protest she didn't snore. It was he who snored. It was a game they played. She was curled up, her knees bent into her flat stomach. Her eyes closed now, her breathing came in short pants, slow and soft. She purred like a cat.

He lifted himself up on his elbow. He sat up. He searched the bed for his underpants. They had moved up underneath her pillow. How was that? He put them on sitting on the bed. He reached for the beside switch. He turned the white switch and the light came on.

She stirred gently. Opened her eyes slowly. She looked at him from the depth of sleep. She smiled, her even teeth glistening. One was pulled out some time ago by a dentist. He took her there, but didn't go in. She said it hurt terribly. And the man wanted to hold her breast.

Slowly she turned, raised herself up. She sat on the bed. She knew the hour, the time. The rites were over. He must go home to his wife. It was always like this.

She slid down the bed and reached for his clothes. He began to put them on. Slowly and carefully. He tied the knot of the tie carefully before the mirror. He put on his coat.

He came near the bed and held her chin. He always did this. It was his parting gesture. He turned. She was still looking at him, looking at his broad back now as he unlocked the door and vanished.

She got up and turned the Yale lock. She came back to the bed. She lay down. Then she heard the car spark. It whined as it backed, and jerked back into first gear, and moved past her door faraway towards his home in the north of the city.

She could not fall asleep immediately. She wasn't thinking of anything in particular. But she was thinking of him. She was always thinking of him.

Then the hours rolled on towards morning. And she fell asleep and dreamed she was dead, and he was alone in the world. Then it wasn't she who was dead, it was he, and she was alone. Then it was the two of them who were dead. They both went to their funeral, to the burial at Awudome. And came home, and slept in each other's arms while people came and looked at the dead people laid in state.

He drove carefully through the deserted Ring Road. Now and then midnight soil removal vans, alias who dey for top, flashed past him scattering their burden on the first lane and perfuming the air with the putrid smell of the city's excrement.

He arrived at his door about three. His watchman was standing near the milkbush, praying to Allah. He had a god.

He inserted his key, entered his hall. There was the smell of cooking long done still lingering. The table was laid for one. He paused to look at the table, adjusted the picture of the Black Mother and her Son above the chest of drawers.

He entered the bedroom quietly. He didn't put on the light lest he wake her up. He took off his clothes, with a deliberation that was boredom. He slipped into the bed beside her. He knew she wasn't asleep.

After about five minutes, she spoke. Where do you come from?

He never answered that question. It was a question that tore through his very soul each time she asked.

After a few more seconds of silence, she spoke again. If you don't love me any more, if that harlot girl is better than I am, and you don't care for me again, tell me and I will go away. I cannot bear the disgrace you are inflicting on me. I cannot. She was raising her voice now. It was always like this, almost every night. She talked on, accused him of every infidelity, and begged for a divorce. Yes, she wanted a divorce.

Then she began to cry and scream. Please, let me go, let me go my own way and you can follow your prostitutes, and the women you think are better than I am. I beg you; I beg you.

He lifted his head up. He picked up his pillow and got up. He groped through the dark for the switch on the wall. He walked slowly out, closed the door gently, and went into the living room. Whenever she became hysterical, he went out into the living room.

There he picked up a cushion from the single armchair. He placed it at the head of the settee. It had no headrest though. Then he lay down on it covering himself with his cover cloth. He tried to sleep. He couldn't. Her voice came through enumerating his crimes, his vileness, his greed, his cruelties, his infidelities, his crimes against her, how she was warned by friends not to marry him, how she rejected other proposals of marriage, and married him against the doubts of her people.

The morning came seeping in gently through the windows. The birds began to stir in the cashew tree outside. Their twittering increased with the brightness of the morning.

He could not sleep. His sleep was sold forever for a love that was within and outside his grasp. For a dream that was unclear. It was at times like this that his headaches would come on. His head would become large, wanting to explode, bells would be ringing in it, and he would want to scream. But he couldn't. He would be floating over a river, flying over a long winding river, awake. The bells would ring louder and louder and louder. And he would pick himself up and step outside into the morning air. He would walk round the milkbush circle about fifty times. He counted every turn. The watchman would be packing his things, rolling his mat and picking up his matchet to go home. He would watch him silently. He had heard Madam screaming, but it was a normal thing. He never interfered. Except the day she broke a china plate over Masa's head. Then he stepped in and led poor Masa away. But Masa was not even aware of the wound on his head. He just stared hard at him and allowed himself to be weakly led outside where he walked round the milkbush circle for a long time, in his cover cloth, and stared. He refused to have the wound washed. Madam packed her things and left. Masa didn't sleep at home for three days. The fourth day, Madam came back brought by her father. And Masa came home.

The sun was breaking through the clouds. It promised to be one of those hot dreary days of sweat and dust and overwork. His headache was going. The bells were still ringing but no longer loudly. The watchman had gone home with his Moslem beads.

Whistling a long-forgotten tune from a hymn about putting one's load by Jesus' side, he walked into his house again to prepare for the day. The bells were faint now. And the headache was gone. He was calm, very calm.

# ••• *Chapter 6a*

Remember the pinewood summers, blue mist descending over the city of Malmö when I stayed with Ernest and his Danish landlord plus his girl Eva of fictitious blonde beauty and the manner of arctic winters. Now the fire exit of lovers' passion is the path through a woman's legs to stare at the moon slanted taking a pee over the ocean. That was the year I noticed the fingerless leper woman clutching a baby unto her bosom on the corner of Pagan Road. Years after she was there, with the same baby, singing her a lullaby in a strange tongue stretching her fingerless hands to passers for coppers for a meal for the two of them.

My brother and I we used to search through the sacred grove of Sofe among shrines where carvers of deities from Abomey, where the thousand gods lived, cut out gods for hidden shrines among tall baobabs.

Death refused to accept money, and insisted on taking man. The carvers – we knew one very well – would look up and stare at us in hostile indifference. We would pretend we were searching for birds and squirrels, and walk by, our eyes scanning tree-tops for figs ripening and weavers in boot nests chatting away dropping a thousand pieces of excrement on brown fallen leaves. They carved deities and dufozi, the pageant of migrations and stories of bravery and the hunt on the journey from Notsie – sometimes they carved men and women with legs suggestively intertwined. When they are done, the drummer leaders will take them out for the out-dooring of great new drums, Oleke, Adzro, Agkebor, Abyssinia, under the blackberry tree on a Sunday in between seasons of sowing of crops and the gathering of the last harvest.

There was Tanya who lived off Leninski Prospect. We met at a party in the brief sojourn in Moscow when we roamed dialectical materialist streets to the tune of 'Moskva Viechera' and spoke Russian phrases of I love you, I will love you till communism engulfs the whole world, till imperialism is dead, till the capitalist hyenas boil in their own blood, till Africa returns to her own. We drank many toasts, it was in the days of Tovarish Nikita Sergeievitch Khrushchev, those glorious days of Soviet toasts – we drank one night I remember seventeen toasts, to Africa, to African unity, to Soviet African solidarity, to the solidarity of all workers in all lands, to . . . everything. Tanya escaped and spent the night in my university room overlooking a dull Soviet park. On the train from Leningrad, Alexander Ivanovich Yuravel, who agreed when I said his name meant a vulture and an eagle in a simultaneous breath, wept bitterly when I said, You Russians are no different. You are like the imperialists. He wept on behalf of the Party and of the Central Committee, and of the General Secretary of the Communist Party of the Soviet Union. We walked through Park Katherina where women milled around while a large band played Dixieland jazz with the anger and the enthusiasm of resurrected demons. I picked my way, danced the rock 'n' roll – it was a taboo in the days when socialist realism frowned heavily on decadent music – but I am an African – long live the Dark Continent. The police came and widened the dancing ring, and me and my partner spoke French, I with an African accent, she with a Ukrainian accent. Alexander rolled home in the arms of two enormous women whom I suspected of being gin-drinking and cigar-smoking lesbians. He said it would be punishment if he went with them.

Stones, oil lamps, rings, landscape flashes, my milkbush is on fire, my people, it is on fire. The yellow lights of streets paved with human excrement from flying trucks pronounce and witness it. Underneath them painted prostitutes are hawking their pussies to Lebanese merchants, cedi a piece with the prospect of dzara, ntosuo, and if you know where they sell penicillin you can buy and buy. The Lido is swinging tonight, brothers, and big men have brought out their harridans; they are in concubinage with them. Soon they – the harridans – will go on European tours, to villas outside Rome and have audience with the Pope. Among the dancers is the man with the golden bed.

The Maharajah of Mysore, a learned gentleman of upper Indian caste, is delivering the Aggrey-Frazer-Guggisberg Memorial Lecture this evening in the Great Hall of the university. His subject is something about the transmutation of the economies of developing countries and the rise of indigenous bureaucracies, mutatis mutandis, theft and robbery in the new revolutionary countries of Africa and Asia. Unbless the cows, dear India. Long live the Third World!

I clutch the bizarre benevolence of my living-room, in the screaming agony of my soul, my body, in a fitful sleep I dream my lover is dead.

The fool I am. She was dead long long ago in her twelfth year.

## ••• *Chapter 7*

They hung around together, the boys from the school up on the hill. School was over. They were expecting the results. One or two got teaching jobs in St Albans College. It is one of the postwar secondary schools that sprang up in the city because serious people felt the educational need of the country, and possessed a sharp nose for smelling quick money. Boys from up country who were eager to learn, whose parents had a little money, but who could not get into the big schools like Achimota and Mfantsipim in Cape Coast, rushed to the new schools, secured lodgings with distant relatives, and bought for a relatively cheap amount some sort of education.

His friend Sammy was the history master from Form One to Five and was also put in charge of sports in the distant hope that the school would one day get its own playing field near the mental hospital.

There were six hundred students who were all day boys; classes were held in Dr Dodu's house. The house was originally built by a man of wealth and a large family. The bedrooms, of which there were eight, were turned into classrooms; toilets were knocked into pantries to provide additional classrooms for the ever growing population of the school. Mr Anokye, a retired pharmacist, owned the school. He laid great emphasis on science, being a science man himself. He wore a small-rimmed pair of glasses which made him look like one of those little black cats on Christmas cards. He had a small voice which squeaked with akpeteshie, and a breath like the smell of gunpowder. He had spent many years at Korle Bu Hospital where he drank the methylated spirit meant to be supplied to laboratory assistants. He was dedicated to learning, a scholar in many ways. He knew Archimedes' principle. Whenever he shouted, during terminal examinations, his battle cry of Eureka! Eureka! then he had caught someone cheating, someone looking over his mate's answer sheet. Mr Anokye came from a long line of scholars. He claimed his grandfather went to England with Reverend T. A. Barnes, D.D., who was the Anglican bishop of Cape Coast Diocese from 1896 to 1909. He was dedicated to his work. He interviewed Sammy himself, questioned him about his parentage and religious background, listened to him carefully, and decided to appoint him on a salary of six pounds per month pending the outcome of his Cambridge School Certificate examination. He questioned him closely on history, especially the Glorious Revolution, and Oliver Cromwell.

This was the job most of the lads secured, in half a dozen schools like St Albans scattered among the slums of the city.

But Amamu was more fortunate. He got a job as a reporter on the *African Sentinel*, the left-wing paper of the Progressive Party. The editor, Mr Zuba, was a man who had climbed up in the profession by sheer will power. He was at the subeditor's desk on the *Daily Echo* in 1932, and claimed that he had worked under the famous West African journalists, Azikiwe and Wallace Johnson. He moved to the subeditor's desk at an increased salary of two pounds a month. Then on to the *Morning Post* in 1937. Obese and slow, Mr Zuba was able to fight the *Post*'s battle singlehanded for, as he claimed, his editor and founder, Mr Samuel, an Accra man, was illiterate. He did work with that benign and empty laugh that characterizes fat people. After years at the subeditor's desk he left because Mr Samuel had refused to grant him an increase. Embittered and disappointed, he pursued Mr Francis Grantley, the Sekondi merchant, to divert a little of his money into establishing the *African Sentinel*. The *Sentinel* was to have a policy based on very powerful slogans directed at the professional people and their class snobbery. The people who should be attacked were the doctors and the lawyers. The snobbery and the superior style of these people should be exposed to public ridicule. Mr Grantley had suffered a number of indignities at the hands of these people. He knew the hell-lot of them, offsprings of harlots who went to bed with European adventurers, and the descendants of slaves from Brazil.

Mr Zuba knew a few socialist phrases – 'proletariat', 'suffering masses', 'the people', 'means of production' were never missing in the *Sentinel*.

One of Amamu's first assignments, he remembered, was to cover the great flood that hit the city in the middle of 1949. The flood had done great damage. People were rendered homeless. They packed their household goods on little rafts while they walked knee deep in water to salvage what had remained of their movable property. The water rushed furiously, carrying along fowls and goats.

One old lady told the story, with tears. It rained heavily at night, her roof was leaking. She kept awake waiting for her daughter to return from town. What work did her daughter do? She didn't know. Suddenly the wooden wall made of packing cases collapsed, and water gushed into the room. She rushed out, but the water was everywhere. She packed her things and put them on the only table. When she went out again on hearing wailings from the next house, the roof collapsed.

They took pictures, wading through the flood. Zuba had already chosen the caption, 'The Plight of the Suffering Masses.' He liked it immensely. A picture of a doctor's house would be a perfect insert. And he himself coming out of the Sea View with enough food to feed ten working-class families in his stomach.

The greatest story he ever did was the story of Sasieme. News had come in from travellers that the village of Sasieme was razed to the ground by the government forces, and the leading men of the village had been arrested for organizing rebellion and riot against the District Commissioner. He was one of a team of one cameraman and an older reporter. They arrived in Sasieme in the evening. Because of the curfew that was in force, they stayed at Ahliha, a village eight miles away. On the morning of the next day, they entered the town. They went straight to the white Superintendent in charge of the riot squad from Elmina to obtain permission. As soon as he knew they were from the *Sentinel* the Superintendent became extremely agitated. He darted his eyes left and right and said something about half-literate fools calling themselves journalists. They explained their purpose and stressed the fact that they were protected by British laws. They were interested only in the facts. They wanted to look around, interview a few people and take pictures. After a few minutes of wrangling and anger on both sides, they were allowed to enter the village, but before that the Superintendent drew their attention to the Riot and Sedition Act.

They entered Sasieme at about ten in the morning. The whole village was deserted. Houses had been burned to the ground. Goats and domestic animals wandered about. Vultures were already feeding on a few bloated carcases in the bypaths. They took quick pictures. There was no one to interview. The riot squad was occupying the Presbyterian School premises. They heard the laughter of women from the classrooms, and groans and thuds from the Headmaster's office which was being used as a temporary cell. They went back to the Superintendent to ask permission to interview some of the elders in the cell.

They interviewed a few of the refugees who had fled to Ahliha. The story was this. When the time came for the villagers of Sasieme to celebrate the Avakpata festival, they applied to the District Commissioner for a permit to hold a durbar and to perform the public rites of cleansing. But the District Commissioner refused to grant them a permit with the excuse that, as the political situation was very tense following the Accra riots and Nkrumah's positive action, a decree had come from the Governor banning all big gatherings. That night the elders of Sasieme held a meeting at the Dufia's house. Their gods and the ancestors of the stool in whose shadow they lived and prospered would be angry if they failed to perform the rites of purification and worship, they said. Where had it been heard before that a people had neglected to honour their gods and cleanse the ancestral stools because the white man said they should not? There were a few fiery speeches. Old men spoke with their heads in their hands. It was agreed that they would cleanse their stools and perform the rites. It was better, they said, to perform their duties by their gods and ancestors and escape the anger of the invisible ones even if they incurred the anger of the white Governor from beyond the seas who apparently didn't have ancestors and stools and didn't understand such matters.

That same night, the town crier announced through the lanes of Sasieme that the Avakpata was around, the priests had seen the owner of the sky seven days ago riding a pure white horse across the sky at high noon. At eight in the morning of the following day, the stool guardians left for the riverside. The whole village gathered under the ancestral odum tree where the first house in Sasieme was built. They were waiting for the return of the guardians of the stool. The Dufia arrived amidst firing of musketry. Dancing went on till nine, when suddenly three of the stool guardians were seen running towards the village. They brought the news that the soldiers and the white commandant came upon them just as they were leaving the riverside. They seized the three ancestral stools and arrested the carriers, Adonu and four others. They were marching towards the village. The elders listened in silence. The Dufia sent for his battle dress, a short smock studded with talismans. Hunters rushed home to fetch their guns. Ten kegs of gunpowder were distributed. Women and children were sent home. Those who had no guns armed themselves with matchets, and the men of Sasieme sat down while the leopard drums sounded in muffled tone.

Meanwhile the District Commissioner upon orders of the Governor had ordered the arrest of the Dufia and the stool fathers for ignoring his instructions. The riot squad was now marching into Sasieme with the captured stools. Their prisoners, who were bleeding profusely from bayonet wounds, were being kicked on the buttocks into the town, some being dragged by the scruff of their necks. The white Superintendent, Robert Perry, was in front. Brought up in a 'home' in Surrey, he grew up tough and martial. As a scholarship student at Oxford he distinguished himself, and when he was called up during the war, he did not hesitate. He saw action in the Mediterranean, and briefly in Normandy. He was sent to Africa after the war, and joined the Gold Coast Police Force, which was badly in need of young men with military experience in those days. He loved his work. Because of his military record, he was moved to the riot squad at Elmina. He had handled a few tricky situations in his time. But this was his major assignment. He was capable of handling the situation.

The soldiers marched into the village square. They saw the elders in battle dress sitting down. A few bold ones were doing a funny war dance with loaded dane guns. The leopard drums went on, wailing mournfully for the gods and the ancestors who were being denied their rites. Superintendent Perry read the riot act and asked the gathering to disperse. The elders sat silent. The drums wailed and mourned the death of the gods and the desecration of the holy stools of Sasieme.

And after a few minutes of silence, Superintendent Perry decided to fire a few shots in the air to frighten the bunch of savages into dispersing. The shots rang out and the blood of the men of Sasieme was whipped into action. Within ten minutes or less the fighting was over. A few of the elders had escaped. Salah, the pig butcher, was seen vaulting the cactus hedge of the Presbyterian School; he vanished under the lemon trees. Three people were killed and five constables were carried away on stretchers with cutlass wounds. By the help of tear gas, the villagers were overpowered and arrested.

The Dufia and the elders of his council were handcuffed and sent to Keta. The less important men were locked in the Headmaster's office where they received occasional blows administered by drunken policemen. The police, pursuing their victory, burned down the village, took captive the women, rounded up stray goats and sheep, looted houses for money and gold trinkets and liquor, and returned triumphantly to the school compound singing a song about the sergeant major's mother's genitals, dragging along some of the village women who could scarcely stand on their feet.

## ••• Chapter 7a

Someone has drawn a flaming cross on the Black Maria; the logic of preventive detention and protective custody; the histrionic vacuity of recent history in which everyone is a silent anchorite worshipping his private god far from the crowd.

Neville was talking about the transformation of quantity into quality in Oxford in the house of Peter, as we sat on the lawn; the other one whom we christened Peter was also there. The revolution must triumph, comrades.

Nkrumah, from all accounts, just continued the work of the British colonialists. Government by force of arms – vis et armis – government by chicanery, tricks, new tricks will be worked out with devastating logic for a one-party state in which colonial activists will attend a meeting where they will collect a guinea per head to build a writers' and artists' home at the beach between the lagoon and the sea in the picturesque village of Botianor. Lectures will have to be organized to explain the African personality, the role of the press, and the importance of creating a new identity, after centuries of colonial rule, slavery and rape. The rape of a continent in darkness.

In the still morning come the gun booms, the muskets are firing volleys of victory into the morning air, as John and Ken rush to my house to tell the news: the heady wine of victory is spilled in the army mess. The intellectuals are getting ready to read brilliant papers on the great subject – WHAT WENT WRONG IN GHANA – barely three months after one of them had lectured to the secret conclave of the Convention People's Party's National Executive on the premises of the great white Elephant Job 600, about I know not what.

We will be caught on this mountain again, dying, screaming, our eyes on heaven. On this dunghill we will search among the rubble for our talisman of hope.

After the government was overthrown, a lot of the fellows came out with bloodcurdling stories of how they were nearly sent into detention, of how they escaped jail by a hair's breadth – what was left was to pledge flinching loyalty – in the words of one of the very learned professors on the hill – to the new regime.

Long Live Ghana.

At the club there was the pathologist with flaming moustache who whispered that the take-over was not as bloodless as put over. But it was bloodless, damn his flashing drum-major-in-mufti moustache. It was like the time when in preparation for independence celebration beggars were herded off into cattle trucks to outlying villages – concentration, detention, custody – to make way for the overseas dignitaries coming to see the new first black nation being born. When the dignitaries left they were brought back and released upon the pavements.

The constabulary are riding grey horses through the market with whips, scream at hawkers who scamper and scatter in the direction of the Arabic school where you can't distinguish the voice of the teacher from the pupils'! The shit vans are rattling down the streets in broad daylight. But the army is in tatters, we must clothe the soldiery first, we must buy them new munitions, and new pips for newly appointed brigadiers and generals. All of it is Nkrumah's fault – the rogue.

As my sight went lower on them, each seemed to be strangely twisted between the chin and the beginning of the chest, for the face was turned towards the loins and they had to come backwards since SEEING FORWARD WAS DENIED THEM.

Dante's *Inferno*. Canto XX

Someday, by some rivers, the elephant grass shall spawn food, the sand of the shores shall grow grain for the granaries to grind into our small pots that will cook for a whole nation to eat.

Word reached me the other day that – no, forget it.

The logic of protective custody is the reasoning of preventive detention is the argument for colonialism. To those who have, more shall be given, and from those who have not, even the little they have shall be taken away. That is the new dialectics.

They are singing obscene songs in the streets today, according to Joe, about a man with a penis like a cannon.

fear death by guns.

## ••• *Chapter 8*

The hymn floated from nowhere. It flowed strong and clear and firm.

I hear Thy welcome voice
Which calls me, Lord, to Thee,
And cleansing in Thy precious blood
Which flowed on Calvary,
I am coming, Lord,
Coming unto Thee.
Wash me, cleanse me in Thy blood
That flowed on Calvary.

The children, dirty and tired from their Saturday noon games on the fig tree, followed the voice. They came round to the corner of the goldsmith shop. There in front of the chemist's shop he stood, his face lifted to the sky and his eyes misty with age.

I am coming, Lord,
Coming unto Thee.
Wash me, cleanse me in Thy blood
That flowed on Calvary.

A few more boys had joined the earlier group, watching the man. A few were still sucking their fingers dripping with the juice of mangoes. He was dressed in a white drill suit, gone grey; around his neck was a pastor's clerical collar battered by time. Under his arm was an old Bible in black binding and the *Pilgrim's Progress.*

I am coming, Lord,
Coming unto Thee.
Wash me, cleanse me in Thy blood
That flowed on Calvary.

The children stood silently as he sang. They were watching. When he finished, he lowered his face and looked at them. Jesus said, Let the children come unto me, my beloved in Christ, so our Lord said. Some say that I am mad. I am not. It is only that I have seen the evil ways of the world!

The children were fidgeting now. He wasn't one of the people they always harassed. They had recently formed a gang which waged war on local lunatics. Their favourite battles were fought with a tall Kabre man who really knew how to throw stones. They had had quite a number of expeditions against him. Then there was Masa the short strong madwoman from across the lagoon. Most of the time they won against their enemies. A few grown-ups had come upon them now and then, and had reported them to their parents. Some were whipped in their homes. But you don't make a juju for a dog which forbids him to touch palm oil. The wars continued.

With this particular one, they weren't too sure. He was gentle and spoke with a quiet voice in the dialect of Lome. But Tokpo was itching to throw a stone. He was bending near a wall. He was collecting broken pieces of pots. The ones that sail the air like birds, and cut as sharp as knives. A few of the boys had seen Tokpo. He was their leader. He normally gave the orders. And they must obey or otherwise face expulsion.

I shall continue to serve the Lord in His vineyard, for the harvest is great but the labourers are few.

Two Sundays ago they had attacked the Faith Tabernacle Church in session at the beach with stones. It was a moonlit night. The tabernaclers gave chase, and two of the boys were caught and sent to the police station where they were given twelve lashes each, on the bare back. He escaped. A few days later, he went back and heard Martha, their leader, preaching with tears in her eyes, and a bandage around her head. He felt as if it was his stone which did that. Then he left after the big prayer when everyone howled and screamed.

The man turned gently in his torn black shoes. He headed towards the Presbyterian Chapel.

I am coming, Lord,

Coming unto Thee.
Wash me, cleanse me in Thy blood
That flowed on Calvary.

The children followed him silently. Then it happened. Tokpo raised their battle cry and the stones flew. The man was surprised momentarily, and after the first hail, he broke into a trot. He headed for the beach. More stones rained on his back.

He alone did not cast a stone. He stood, trapped like an animal. He could hear the shout of his comrades, as they chased their enemy into the Presbyterian Mission Compound.

The Reverend Paul Dumenyo was born in the hilly country of northern Togoland during the period when the country was under German occupation and the Christian missionaries from Bremen had started their evangelical work there. His father, Jonathan Dumenyo, was one of the early converts to be baptized, and taught to read and write, and finally became a catechist. He was converted with a number of slaves who were bought and given their freedom by the missionaries; among them was Aaron Kuku, who later became a great Christian in Eweland. Paul's mother did not take to Christianity early, but at her marriage to the catechist she was baptized into the Evangelical Presbyterian Church. Paul's father was over forty when he married Adzoyo, who was later christened Rebecca. After years of waiting, they were blessed with a son. The child was baptized Paul David Dumenyo; the whole of the little convert community knew that he was destined to serve the Lord and take the Gospel to the unfortunate brethren of the interior. So Paul grew up in the fear and knowledge of the Lord. He started at the mission school when he was five. Everything went well. He was confirmed barely a month when confusion broke open. That was in 1914. The missionaries called the converts one evening hurriedly. After prayers and supplications to the Lord, it was announced that Germany was at war and the British and French forces from the Gold Coast and Dahomey had arrived in Togoland. Only the good Lord knew what would happen. As for themselves, they had no apprehension but their fear was what would happen to the seeds of the church they had begun to nurse and tend. The fate of the small Christian church was in the balance. Then the elders of the church, especially the old women, including Paul's grandmother, baptized Sarah, shed tears with the missionaries and commended one another to the infinite care of the Lord who was merciful, who sent His only begotten son, Jesus Christ, who died to save them all from sin.

The next morning the British and the French forces arrived; they surrounded the hill station and made the missionaries prisoners, amidst the tears and the prayers of the church members.

The future looked grim. Catechist Jonathan Dumenyo gave word and the congregation assembled in the chapel.

Dearly beloved in Christ, what shall we do? Then the Christians burst into fresh tears. Paul, about fifteen years old, wept with the devout elders.

However, the little community settled down and the education work of the mission continued in spite of the difficulties. Those who knew something already learned more in order to teach. Paul was among the first crop of teachers at the station. He read his Bible many times over, and he loved the *Pilgrim's Progress.* A Sunday school was started at which it was read chapter by chapter every Sunday. Paul took his work seriously; on Sundays he walked to neighbouring villages where church work had started in earnest. His busiest times were the feasts, especially Palm Sunday and Easter when he led the small village route marches, waving palm branches, into the hill station for his father to preach the sermon.

Then the war ended. Germany was defeated. The Christians knew that their friends from Bremen would never come back. But the work of the Lord continued. The French administration came. Then the Roman Catholics who had a Papa in Rome, and burned incense in sacraments which they carried on the road whenever the rains were late. The mission grew, however, liaised with the growing mission in Keta and Amedzofe in the Gold Coast.

Paul grew up in this bustling atmosphere of church work in the fear, love and knowledge of the Lord. He was twenty-five. His superiors saw his work, devotion and singleness of purpose, and at the synod meeting in Lome they decided to ordain him along with other energetic Christians whose life and work in the service of the Lord had already won them respect and honour among their own people.

The ordination ceremony in Lome, the eighth of December 1926, was attended by church members from the hill station, and by Christians from as far as Akropong in the Gold Coast. There were as many as ten priests who officiated. The Church of God a Kingdom is, a mystic harmony. An atmosphere of intense piety and Christian fellowship marked the ceremony. Paul's mother burst into tears. His father, it pleased the Lord, was not there to see his son received into the arms of the Church. He had died the year before of typhoid fever and a complicated hernia.

The young priests were assigned to various stations. Paul was sent to Atakpame where mission work had grown heavy and a young and energetic pastor was needed.

The mission house stood on a hillock overlooking a small garden planted with pawpaws, pears and bananas by the devout Christians in readiness for the new pastor. Paul was met at the outskirts of the town by the elders including the chief's linguist, who had also embraced Christianity. With hymns, the most popular being, 'He Whom God Loves, Him He Sends Far Afield', the procession entered the village. The new pastor wore a bright white drill suit and clerical collar, white like a ram's crest. He had a smile for everyone. In the little chapel, he preached his first pastoral sermon about a people who lived in darkness but received the light of the Lord, and praised the Lord for the achievements of the past. He commended his new parishioners to the love and care of the Lord, through Jesus Christ our Lord, Amen.

Paul plunged into his work with the zeal of the Lord. He reorganized the church work, he allotted time for cathechismal education and itinerant preaching in the neighbouring villages. After two weeks catechism classes began in earnest, on Mondays and Fridays at six-thirty in the evening. The enrolment was encouraging, twenty young men and women formed the first group of new converts. He administered the Lord's Supper, Baptism and Confirmation. He was well liked by his parishioners.

His mother wrote to him one day:

Dear Son,

When you left us, we were all sad. But the Lord Himself will protect you, guide your feet in the path of righteousness, as you are engaged as a labourer in His vineyard.

There is a little matter. I think it pleaseth the Lord that you should take unto yourself a wife. This is necessary if your work will not be hampered by the snares of the Evil One. I and your uncles have thought about it. We decided that you should take your cousin Ruth to wife. She is a good girl, devout and steadfast in the Lord. She has just passed Standard Seven, and has sat at the Lord's Supper. She is a good girl. Write to us. As to the wedding you can arrange it with your superiors in Lome.

I commend you to the Lord. Our corn harvest this year was very good, thanks to the Lord, we are in good health.

I remain

Your mother

Rebecca Dumenyo

Paul read his mother's letter many times over. He had not thought about marriage. Of course the Church enjoins its servants to marry because it eases the Lord's work. Didn't Christ himself officiate at the marriage at Cana, and liken the Church unto a bride? He gave the matter a second thought. The next day he wrote to his mother.

Dear Mother,

Thank you very much for your letter. I am aware of your good intentions in the matter of my marriage; for the Lord Himself enjoins us to take wives unto ourselves and promote the work of the Church. I am therefore in full agreement.

I shall write to my superiors in Lome and seek their guidance and help in this matter.

I do not remember my cousin Ruth. But your commendations about her please my heart. I am sure that the Lord Himself was the one who guided you in your choice.

His work here is proceeding at a good pace. New converts join our ranks every day. Praise be to Him.

Give my greetings and blessings to all at home. I need your prayers.

I remain

Your son

Paul

Among his catechism pupils was a young girl who had already chosen the name Naomi. She was a lively girl, full-breasted with rings on her neck. She had a quick brain and learned her lessons very fast.

The first time Paul noticed her, she was looking into the pastor's eyes. Their eyes met. Paul shifted his at the same time as she did. After that day he could not look into the girl's eyes whenever he asked her questions. Paul was troubled. He prayed the Lord to let the cup pass away. For he knew that in his heart something which you cannot describe was growing. In the night when it seemed as if the Lord had heeded his prayers, he slept peacefully only to await eagerly the coming of Friday so that he could set eyes on Naomi.

She also noticed the pastor's attitude had changed towards her. He asked her fewer questions, and could not look into her eyes. She was a grown-up girl, and had already known a man. She liked the pastor very much.

Things went this way for two weeks. Paul bore his torment like a soldier of Christ. The girl saw the pastor in her dreams. He touched her.

One Sunday evening, the second Sunday after Pentecost, Paul sat in his room preparing catechism lessons. He heard a knock on the door. The woman who cooked for him had already brought the food and gone. It could be Absalom, one of the pupils from the mission school who had volunteered to wash his things and iron them.

He went to the door and opened it. At first he could not recognize who it was in the dark because he had just left the brightness of the hurricane lamp. After a few seconds he realized it was a woman. Naomi.

Come in, come in, Naomi. Are you alone?

The girl nodded, her gaze fixed on the floor.

Did you walk alone in this night, dear Sister?

She nodded again. Paul pointed to a chair. She sat down. Her eyes were still fixed on the floor. Paul was worried. His heart was beating fast. Assuming a casual friendly tone, he asked, Now, now, what can I do for you? Are you in trouble?

No, Pastor, we made some tapioca and some ground nut stew. I thought I should bring you some.

She pulled out from under her cloth a pan wrapped in a clean white embroidered napkin. Paul got up and received the gift.

Thank you very much, Naomi.

Do not mention it. It is our duty to look after you. I don't think Auntie Dora cooks very good food for you.

Oh well, she does her best, she is very good.

They were sitting down now, in silence. The lamp was burning weakly, now and then flickering. The kerosene was at its lowest. Paul began to tremble slightly and there was a buzzing noise in his ears. After what seemed to be a year of silence, he plucked up courage to ask:

How are your catechism lessons? Are you finding difficulty with them?

No, Pastor. I like them very much. I learn very fast.

You do well.

Silence. The kerosene was finishing. Paul went into the bedroom and groped under the bed for the kerosene bottle. He came back, poured some oil into the lamp, stealing furtive glances at Naomi.

Do you know which parable tells of the lamp?

Oh yes, the parable of the ten virgins. I enjoy it very much.

After a brief and absent-minded Biblical conversation, Naomi told him of her people, who were farmers, and she herself had stayed in Lome with an aunt who made bread.

Soon the wind outside began to whistle in the pawpaw and the mango trees. A storm was brewing. Paul rose up.

I think you must hurry back. I shall take the raincoat.

He entered the bedroom, and lighting his torch he unhooked the mackintosh from the mosquito pole and turned round. He bumped into Naomi, who had followed him into the bedroom.

Paul's catechism class the following day was a torment. He

wrote notes to Naomi, telling her how he loved her only as a sister in Christ, and how she should not come to him again, supplicated and pleaded with the Lord on their behalf.

The following Sunday Naomi came. After that she came every Sunday evening.

Paul gave up the struggle with the Devil, and prayed for forgiveness. He went through his pastoral duties with the listlessness of a lost dog.

Four months passed. Naomi left Atakpame to visit her aunt in Lome.

Paul resumed correspondence with his mother about his marriage. Everything was arranged. He went home.

On the second Sunday after Epiphany, church bells rang in Atakpame. The parish was getting ready to attend the marriage ceremony of their beloved pastor. Two pastors came from Lome. The last bell had just gone.

The small chapel was decorated with palm fronds and flowers. A new altar cloth covered the altar.

O perfect love, all
Human thoughts transcending,
Lowly we kneel in
Prayer before Thy throne.

The service was half-way through, when the cry of a woman was heard from the rear of the chapel. It was Naomi. She was pregnant with a long belly. Her sobs filled the chapel now as she walked in the little path, as if she was mad, moaning, I am bearing his child, ao, ao, I am bearing his child, my fathers, I am bearing his child. On reaching the foot of the altar, she cast herself on the floor, and wept now as though she was released from all restraints.

When he turned the bend into the mission compound, the children had stopped throwing the stones. He walked into the chapel and knelt down in front of the altar. His forehead was swollen from a stone.

When he emerged, marching towards the lorry station, the little boy was still standing on the corner, the stone he had picked up which he could not cast still in his hand.

I am coming, Lord,
Coming unto Thee.
Wash me, cleanse me in Thy blood
That flowed on Calvary.

The hymn flowed through the din of sparse traffic. The little boy still stood wondering. He threw the stone into the gutter, turned round and walked towards home. The hymn still flowed, now in his head alone.

## ••• *Chapter 8a*

> Audiam quid loquatur in me Dominus Deus;
> quoniam loquetur pacem in pleban suam;
> et super Sanctos suos, in eos qui convertuntur
> ad cor.
>
> Kyrie et Gloria

Be blessed by him in whose honour you are to be burned. Amen. There is a fat man who speaks in a small piping voice and lives in the shadow of the Church of St Peter and St Paul. For the Sunday service, he takes his bath promptly on Saturday evening and sits down to wait for Sunday to make his confession at evening benediction and eat of the body and blood – transubstantiation is not a myth – of Christ. They say he is a eunuch. Christ too was.

The Presbyterian Church faces the outskirts of town, a small broken-down mud shack with iron sheet roofing without a choir run by a drunken catechist who is spending his fiftieth year in the Lord's vineyard for the harvest is good but the labourers are few.

In between lies the banana grove with ripening fruits supervised by the old caretaker suffering from chronic asthma, whose daughter has gone prostituting in the capital these seven years. At Easter she comes home to make a new set of gold trinkets by the goldsmith with oversize testicles and a squint who, rumour has it, has cohabited with his eldest daughter and fathered his own grandchildren.

The first crops were sown in this land by the lonely exiles from Bremen who defied native taboos and rode horses into the sacred town against the expressed dictates of the sky-god, the rider on a white horse in heaven. They died here. They were caught, penned, and fed on raw cassava.

There was a woman at a cocktail party balancing a glass of champagne amidst a group of slanderous wellwishers rushing towards me to push her snout into my face to inquire about your health. It was the day we waged war upon the noisy Apostolic Church near the Indian almond tree, my tree, and chased the lunatic priest who was screaming, Destroy this temple, and I shall build it after three days, and vanished among the crowd at Lome station. The boys rushed shouting, He is here, he is here: I cast down my stone and went home to my mother's house with the coconut tree and the salt-water well. Then I heard the long anguished ululation of the funeral procession from the Holy Trinity Cathedral where the choir was rehearsing the Messiah winding towards Osu Cemetery. The General is dead. The General is dead, and the nation is weeping. The soldiers are marching in the streets behind the gun carriage on which the casket containing the General's body is drawn to the firing of gun salutes to hasten him upon his decaying way.

I remember him very well. Soft and gentle, he wore a T-shirt as we drank whisky. He drank orange from a tall yellow glass.

We cast our stones aside and raced to where they stored gunpowder near the hut of the Kabre man who delighted in stone battles. Soon a seventy-year-old man was arrested and arraigned before the magistrate on a charge of throwing stones into a house at Osu. Seventy years and throwing bricks.

Joe said time was a hermaphrodite offering the therapy of God and we must bend down, lie down and receive our divine medication at his/her hands.

When Pilate asked, What is truth, it should not be believed, as some theological commentators would like us to believe, that he was being irresponsibly facetious. The man was an arm of the Empire, and in a profession such as his, the luxury of a joke is an unthinkable piece of idiocy – an ill-considered act of suicide.

So the General's casket moves from the Holy Trinity Cathedral. The women are weeping copious tears into their dark mourning cloth on this bright sharp morning of a burial. The soldiers have barred the gates against intruders, anarchists and possible incendiarists who may be carrying dangerous bombs to throw at the funeral cortege. Then they played the last post as distinctively as I heard it in *From Here to Eternity* in the committal of body to earth.

Dust to dust, ashes to ashes. The General is Dead. Sipping his orange he asked what our opinions were about the body politic, what must be done. Lenin also wrote copious letters from afar spelling out what was to be done long before his revolution went astray. All revolutions must go astray. That is divine justice.

In the sky the birds assumed the pose of angels in the illustrated Bible flying over the General's body to the grave. The women; poor poor women. They are still weeping.

A man was caught by the soldiers that morning hot-footing it to his home town. That was before Jimmy came back and said he was destined to govern and took a job as a major-domo, an amanuensis in a big powerful department issuing press releases on the conduct of state affairs. A big chief, with a natural hectoring manner, was swearing at the police station that he was forced into the Party, against his will.

Martha, who has chosen the best part, was the spiritual leader of the Apostolic Church near the beach. The congregation was made up of women wanting children, derelict alcoholics who had drunk away family fortunes, and half-wits from a big household where, rumour has it, the men sleep with their own sisters and beget imbeciles.

Someone's name is Jesus, he has life.
Jesus, Jesus, he has life.

They are praying now, in tears and supplication, about Jesus the Saviour, about sin and heaven, life and death, over the General's funeral cortege from the Holy Trinity. My almond tree was in bloom in May flowering with leaves large and flowers like thin fingers of okra being marketed by the Jewish shopkeeper on Kilburn High Road where Michael and I buy African food. Jahn said our food is the colour of our national flags.

In Kensal Rise, the Ghana government has bought a piece of land to be used as burial ground for Ghanaians who die in England. It's very well kept with a tidy white gate and a caretaker who opens and shuts the gate mostly in winter when the stream of mourners enter and depart through the slush.

Microphones are carrying the funeral service to us under the nim trees.

And my lunatic priest has vanished on the road to Lome.

## ••• *Chapter 9*

He was very calm this morning. There was a sudden quiet that surrounded him, like the peace of all times; his heartbeat he would hear against the bedclothes as he tried to sleep the fitful sleep of late mornings after troubled nights. The clock on the dressing table ticked. The air conditioner hummed its eternal hymn.

He opened his eyes. The morning light had come in. With a jerk he raised himself up. He was not thinking of anything in particular. It was just the beginning of one of those ordinary days on which nothing happens. A grey bright day of sunshine and noise.

He went to the office at about eleven. He couldn't stay. He drove to the club. A few faithful members were there, drinking their beer silently. Richard stood behind the counter, polishing a couple of old jugs. The conversation was limping. Each one had a problem. Everyone does at this time of the month.

He drove away not having said a word to anyone. By now they would be discussing him. That he was a funny man. Suddenly he decided he must go to a night club this evening. He would call Sammy. He always knew where a good band was playing.

There was a band from the Congo playing at the Tiptoe. He would go and pick up Adisa. She was not at home.

They drove, he drove, windingly, and he talked all the time. Sammy knew his moods. He was silent. Now and then he muttered something about minding the road. This was the booze time of day, to watch oncoming cars, the open-air gutter on the left. He ignored all these. They turned into the new Ring Road from Seventh Avenue among the nims. They headed towards the Circle. Cars sped past. Some came from behind, swerved in an arc, pulled by their side; the driver said something about their mothers' genitals in Ga.

You had to live long enough to understand women, he said.

Sammy never replied to his monologues. He was a bachelor, not out of choice, but out of the inability to persuade any girl to marry him. He was not serious, they all said. So he was never serious with them. But he was his best friend. From olden days, they used to say. Before he went to England to study law. They were old friends. Sammy went to the university at home. He read a degree in English. He was now working in the Ministry of the Interior as an Assistant Secretary. His job was files. He read about ten a day, minuted instructions to his superiors and inferiors in his impeccable English and got promoted regularly with fifty pounds increase annually. At twenty-three, he clung to his bachelor joys with the tenacity of an acolyte.

They swerved into the pot-holed road where Tiptoe was. Tiptoe was a leftover from the wartime night clubs which catered for the soldiers. It was open-air, like the gutters of the city. There was a thin line of sheds that ran against the wall. On the northern side was a two-storey building whose tenants opened their windows to watch the dancers. There was a man in a small booth, protected by a wire gauze, who gave you a ticket. In the middle of the dance if you wanted to go out, he stamped your palm. This you showed at the gate on return.

As they got out of the car, an army of urchins emerged swarming from the darkness. They were screaming at the same time: Masa, I watch de car. Me, me, masa. Sammy selected a bright-eyed one in half a shirt. You look after the car, O.K? Yes sah. The boy gave a mock salute and turned to his comrades with a swagger. He had done them out of business.

A policeman, perhaps awakened by the noise, walked over. Masa, you must not park here, sah. Sammy tossed him a two-shilling piece and said, You too look after the car, eh?

Yes sah, masa, tank you.

Tiptoe was packed. The Congolese band was on the stand. Every table was taken. A tall fair coloured boy came up, chewing gum in his mouth.

Hey, Rafik, get us a table quick.

Yes, Masa Sammy. Tonight plenty people come here. But go try get table for fine place.

They stood at the edge of the dance floor, looking at the dancers swaying to the music. Rafik came back. He had found a table. But it was near the urinal. Sammy stared at him in disbelief.

Rafik, you fool o, go call Aboud. What!

Rafik came back with Aboud, a fat smiling Lebanese who owned the joint.

O, lawyer, ibi you? I no sabe ibi you. O, Rafik, you fool proper. You come give lawyer and him friend table near piss house? I no see someone fool like you before. Please, lawyer, come, follow me.

They were now comfortably seated at the edge of the floor. The proprietor had sent them two large glasses of scotch. He knew lawyer very well. He was his friend.

You seen Adisa?

No.

The band had picked up a cool pachanga. One of the amplifiers was right behind them. It was a five-piece with two guitars, drums, a bass, a conga set, and a half-caste singer who had a face like he was the darker brother of Elvis Presley. They had struck up 'A Léopoldville, comment parle pas Français'. A mixture of Lingala and French, a number which was very popular in those days. The music massed through its own beat reminiscent of the slow agbekor music, whirling in a steady syncopation. The guitars were whining away with every beat. The amplifiers carried the rhythm right into your heartbeat, and the rhythm and your heartbeat became one in consonance with the movement of the dancers. The girls in their tight-fitting dresses, their bodies contouring around the rhythmic waves from every heartbeat and every footfall, away from the boys who stamped and beat the floor with their manhood, sweating generously in their sweaters and leather jackets. Amamu kept his eyes on the entrance. Adisa would come in one day. The drums told their old story. A female and a male mating in rhythm in the order and sequence of the sacred love act. The beat of every inch of leather transfigured through the amplifiers wailed through the heartbeat and the footfall of everyone, wailed upstairs in an echo that hit the big forget-me-not tree that stood squarely between the urinal – the piss house – and the bar, swaying in the transfiguration.

Ka dzin kon kon ka dzi

Ka dzin kon kon ka dzi
   Ka dzi
   Ka dzi
Kon ka kon ka kon ko
   Kon ko . . . Kon ko
Ka dzin kon kon ka dzi

The girls had now caught the rhythm from the echo, and made it their own, part of their bodies, part of their waists, then breasts and their buttocks, jumping in consonance, in oneness and separateness of the love act which the drums initiated and of which they knew and had been part of since conception.

The drums plucked up a new tone higher and higher, angry now, thrusting, throbbing in sequence straying away from the echo a second in separation, holding the girls in their embrace, and loving them and loving them in beats and they loving back in an ecstasy which only is love's.

Ko ko ko dzin
Ka kan ka kan
Kan kan kan
Ko ko ko kan kan
Kan ko ko kan

Then it came down, the beat now preparing to release the girls from that intimate embrace. The drums were doing the after-act of cleansing, to allow the guitars to take over and do their low after-love caressing, moaning and unsatisfied wanting more. The drums complaining in low monotones, separate now, leaving the love chambers for the newcomers to share the beginning of the sequence, the new act.

There she is . . . there she is.

Who?

Adisa.

It was Adisa. She stood by the entrance. She was looking around.

Don't let her see you.

It looked as if she was alone. She was dressed in a grey silver frock which shone gently in the dimness of the dance floor. Her eyes were scanning the whole place, the band and the dancers, and those who sat wedged far away between the forget-me-not tree and the urinal, and those who perched on the bar stools.

Adisa came from the north. She possessed the silence and the quiet of the savannas, the smell of fresh earth upturned for the millet season in her native home. Her skin was the darkness of silent northern rivers which do not dry up, though they are not tributaries.

She and Amamu had met, a year ago, in court. There was a fight among the girls at the Lido. The police van came and took all of them to the station at Adabraka. She spent the night fighting the constable on duty who came into her cell with his fly open. The next day they were hauled before the magistrate. She went to court in her working clothes, a red velvet low-necked frock that showed a quarter of her breasts. He saw her and heard her silent defiance of the law among her friends. There were six of them. Four were old, the sixth was an infant of fourteen. He defended them.

She stood on the edge of the dance floor now. She saw a girl.

Hey, Rose, you said you would come and call me.

Oh, Adisa, I had to go to the seamstress and . . .

The two girls stood looking at each other. They moved towards a table. One of the boys gave her his chair; she sat reaching for her bag.

He was humming an indistinct tune. His hands fastened around the last drop of scotch as he stared at her.

The Congolese boys struck a slow number, a cool cry which told of a faraway country, about black people, about love, tears and death. The guitars came into their own, twanging in interrupted silences, vibing that story no one and everyone understood. It was a blind man's song, demanding and searching. The singer took over as the strings returned.

In that lonely house
Where darkness engulfs all
Stood Maria.

Then the chorus took over, in a controlled outburst, they retold the tale.

It will be over
When the chains are smashed,
When the tears are wiped away.

Aboud came to the table.

Eh, lawyer, drink i finis? Hei, Rafik, bring lawyer an im friend some whisky.

Amamu got up from his chair. Adisa was dancing to the blind man's song with a short stocky man. He walked towards them. Sammy sat silent, a prayer on his lips. Then he saw them coming to the table. Adisa, bright-eyed, silent, Amamu, a distantly satisfied look on his face.

# ••• Chapter 9a

City nights; the crier on top of the mosque calling the faithful to worship. There is only one God, Allah, and Mohammed is His prophet. City nights, night soil vans scattering suburban excrement on the dual carriageway. One killed a young army officer one dawn, smashed him; they had to extricate his mangled body from among a pile of excrement. Fear death by shit trucks.

A line-up of prostitutes is being inspected by management early tonight before the band takes the stand, before the clients arrive. At the gate, street urchins in rags are rushing to point out parking spaces to serious drinking gentlemen out on the town. A woman is quarrelling venomously with a beggar – professional, mind you – who wants to cheat her over the sale of one stick of cigarette.

Give us a sign. No sign shall be given to you except the sign of Jonah.

At the ninth hour the bands shall strike the forgotten tune redolent of lost villages and age-old rituals carried on the head of stilt-walkers into cities within cities, 'I shall make Nima a city within a city'.

Gay girls in tight silk clothes worn knee length chaperoned by garlicked Lebanese chattering animatedly in Arabic and Pidgin from huge American cars purchased with loans from the national banks of free and independent Africa. Some long-limbed like shy gazelles of the savanna, their lips coated in blood.

A man was caught behind the public latrine at the lorry park cohabiting with a ten-year-old girl selling ground nuts. Statutory rape. When questioned he said it was a slip of the penis.

I met Eduardo in the old battered hotel in Algiers, the capital of the land of a million martyrs, his eyes ablaze with the revolution. A bomb would shatter him in a villa near a lake near his homeland when he was preparing an address to the elders.

In the joyless winter days here, I am walking the streets looking for Lewis Nkosi's white-skinned Negro, fictitious as angels. On the train from Kingsbury an Irish drunk is swearing in fluent Dutch. David will drive me in a blind maze of whiskied vision like a fury looking for my house at 4 A.M. Just when the band boys will be packing up for the dawn.

It is a land of laughing people, very hospitable people. That's what the tourist posters proclaim. They forgot to add that pussy is cheap here, the liquor is indifferent, and the people suffer from a thousand diseases, there are beggars on the tarmac at the airport, and the leaders of government, any government, are amenable to fine financial pressures of undetermined favours.

Lionel was talking about riding the first tank into Johannesburg when the revolution comes. My head erect like that of Conrad's Nigger of the Narcissus, I walk the noon through Covent Garden in search of the theatre where *Niggers Everywhere Arise* is playing. I carry my 'repulsive mask of a nigger's soul' into a pub on Tottenham Court Road with Roger: when I snapped my fingers in remembrance of what I wanted to say, the publican with yellow teeth barked, I am not a dog. No sir, you are not a dog. I am. The dog that died.

Swinging, our nation's pentagon smashes the bludgeoned heads of orphans for a balancing trick of stability.

That there is such a thing as strength of will which is able to haul up so exceedingly close to the wind that it saves a man's reason even though he remains a little queer.

Kierkegaard

That's a blatant lie. Down in the dance hall tonight, a child will scream on his mother's back, Please, Mother, I want to go to heaven. Mother, please. Lovers are doing the pachanga in the joyful way in which Zeke said Africans dance. Natural sense of rhythm. The moralist politician is calling for a moral revolution. It is rumoured that he was once caught cohabiting with . . . someone else's wife. When Luther screamed that reason is the Devil's harlot, he nailed his ninety-nine theses on a door.

One chief went on a Moral Rearmament trip. He came home screaming in the headlines about how decadent the society was becoming, how children were disobedient to their parents and teachers, and small boys were not respecting their elders.

In our walled world of indolent anger, the Saviour walks among us, his heart in a sling.

And these signs shall follow them that believe. The distant city noises recede far away into the fields where Jimmy crashed his car trying to kiss a girl beyond the blue hills. My hands offer nothing. Father had a sign posted on his wall beside the one proclaiming, 'Christ is the head of this House'. On it is written, 'Nothing in my hands I bring'. He used to sing a song when we were little boys about the six feet of earth making us all of one size. One night he fought an up-country driver with a limp who owed him money – five shillings it was he owed. When he was about to crack Father's head with a crowbar the police came and arrested both of them for conduct prejudicial to public peace and order. They spent the night in jail. He came home in the morning, his evening's dinner still on the table, rice and stew, dark as a rain cloud daring anyone to ask him a question. Shortly after thieves came and cut my mother up. They slashed her arm, the arm with which she covered me in my sleep. There was wailing and crying in the grey dawn. And I was covered every inch in my mother's red blood.

Infinite resignation is that shirt we read about in the old fable. The thread is spun with tears, the cloth bleached with tears, the shirt sewn with tears.

Kierkegaard

As much as love, perhaps, with which we can face our Maker to demand the purpose of it all, the reason of it all. The blandly silly hills smoking in an afternoon rain, the putrefaction of earth in decaying nim leaves proclaim a simple solution: Despair and Die.

Maybe I know somewhere where platinum trees grow blossoming in flowers of iron and steel in the factory where someone stayed behind at closing time singing at the top of his voice. We need flowers, gay as those in my butterfly fields to make garlands for our leaders, civilians, soldiers and all, all our leaders plus our natural rulers, signatories to the bond of 1844. Then they will perform the dance of death for us to the music of electric guitars and drums studded with skulls outdoored from old ancestral shrines. They will dance all night in the city halls, in front of drunken foreign dignitaries, a slow dance of death. When the drums and the electric guitars stop, the banquet hall shall be flooded in light and flowers; a little girl shall take a bow before the chief leader, who will be trying desperately to suppress a fart. He is seriously concerned about the moral decay of the nation.

Memory dry as the legs of old women shall proclaim the shame of the crocodile as the shame of the alligator on the day of the lion.

A man in the last throes of syphilis is screaming in a public latrine: It is coming!!

I will get away into the shadow of my tree to await the epiphany of my woman of the sea with hard nipples rippling on the waves parted by moon slash. And she will dance for me even though Neville said, She will not dance again in our time in the paling seasons among the hills of spice. He always sang of the season of pimentos for poverty struck a blow at rich men and they had to sell their cloths to the Lagosian dyers with blue palms.

In the grey truce of these hours we will win a temporary respite. In our penance hour, we shall pack our bags ready for a long journey homewards. And we will not speak in parables any more. For we have acquired the discretion of cowards, and from the compound of our houses we will point to the sky with an oath. As the T.V. set starts kaleidoscope, university dons are going to discuss the problems of developing nations, a notion which the Maharajah found disturbing to state.

Experts will plan our cities, and remove the shit vans from the streets so that dancers at the Lido may not be offended as our world dissolves into a confusion of tangled legs beneath old gaslit lamps at the street corners. Our preferences will be stated unequivocally. There is only one possibility: Despair and Die.

Father came home drunk as a native chieftain singing a song about the Empress Sophia. Your dinner is ready, said Mother. I am not hungry, I am NOT HUNGRY.

And this earth, my brother, shall claim me for her own. Tonight there is a deep silence in the land. Joe says it is the hush hour before the holocaust: it is the silence of death. Children in their green age are pummelling a rag-made Judas on the beach in the ebony night awaiting the moon to rise under my Indian almond. He betrayed their Saviour for thirty pieces of silver.

When the news comes that Verwoerd is shot, Abraham gets irretrievably drunk screaming, The Revolution is here! When the freedom armies return home and lay down their arms, and victory is won, and the leaders make their tearful speeches in the Arena, there will be let loose among the crowd a thousand grey hunting Upper Voltaic dogs, and the struggle for LIBERTY shall enter its second and most gruesome phase.

Slow husago drums are beating as the search goes on for the spirit of the dead priest by the wayside under fallen shrubs in banana groves. Three of the leaders shall hang in the market place in Kinshasa. The conundrums must be solved by their inventors. And with illuminating logic, solutions shall be produced in Constituent Assemblies where the honourable member for Manso west will plead with tears that the use of contraceptives be spelled out and entrenched in the constitution, and an amendment provided that no tyrants or rubber-stamp Parliament can change the clause without a national referendum to be clearly won by an overwhelming majority. The chiefs of the village of Noyi sent a telegram congratulating the Assembly for its sagacity, good sense and patriotism. A nation is doing the death dance now in a banquet hall of its imaginings, proclaiming its salvation with trumpets, the trombones of God take over the sound in heaven – and Christ screams upon the cross, Father, into Thy hands I commend my spirit.

In those medical hours of clinic work the smell of ether controls the earth and men mounted on Sudanese horses scamper around the turf at one forty-five for the grey silver cup. The announcement will be made about those who win a place at the banquet table. Dancing girls shall be released among the crowd, half-naked breasts flapping to the beat of husago drums, searching for ether sodden opiates under medicinal shrubs. The judge shall hit the gavel on the table and declare the mart open. The buyers and the sellers are one.

I shall run all the way home.

I refused the drink she offered in gloved hands a long cigarette holder in her mouth inquiring, Are there fishes in your home town? She was sent to Europe on state funds to learn how to appreciate antiques. Breathless as a long-distance runner she whispers an obscene suggestion about doing fun things on a double bed. I don't, I said. Really?

Willows hang over Peter's cottage into the appled lawn of green where Neville's children are playing cricket. They are half West Indian and understand the rhythmic twirls of Gary Sobers at Lords.

My girls are asleep now. Do not disturb. Fellows are whispering darkly around the circle about the workman who was taken for dead near Awudome Cemetery. The man hadn't eaten for three days. When the Sanitary Department's burial cart came to collect him to the hospital for a post-mortem and thence to his final resting place he protested like Lazarus from the grave that he was NOT DEAD. He was only HUNGRY. They bought sixpenny worth of rice and stew for him. When he finished eating he brushed his gown and walked home to Nima, muttering Niniana, which means, Your mothers.

We shall arrive in the evening hour when the rites shall be over, when the hungry of the land shall be given food – they will snatch it from sacred shrines of dead ancestors if need be. We shall recall the vision of the dancing girls performing the steps of the departed among the fields of thorn. The rattler's eloquence shall be pitted against the resonance of ancestral drums, amulets shall talk of divinations unheeded.

I took my love home tonight. She was silent. We sat facing each other on her broken-down sofa and talked for hours in silence.

Then we knew the true respite cannot be won. The verdict is a simple one, a dangerous lie that must be lived to the end. Keep silent and let me pay the price.

Despair and Die.

## ••• *Chapter 10*

Months before all that, his wife came home. She had stayed behind in London when he came home. He had married a Cape Coast girl, the daughter of a retired judge of the Supreme Court.

She came home one morning late in June. The B.O.A.C. plane was touching down at eleven. There was a crowd at the small airport. People were crawling over one another in the sweat and smell of the small enclosure. Alice's relatives were there in white cloth. Her father stood near the clerk's desk in a striped suit of the mid-thirties, grey-haired and pleased. Amamu walked over to greet his in-laws.

Good morning, sir.

Good morning. Where is your father?

He hasn't been well, Pa. He has the flu.

It's the weather. There is a virus flu going round. Many people are going down with it.

The hum of milling women chatting each other up on every subject. The airport clerks, important at their posts, running up and down with serious-looking folders. The voice of the airways girl came over the microphone:

B.O.A.C. flight 217 from London is delayed for about one hour. Arrival time will now be twelve noon local time.

The clerks looked more important now that the announcement had been made. The superintendent in charge stood in the corner near the B.W.A. kiosk, his khaki shining, playing with his baton.

The arrival hall in its shabbiness hummed with human activity. It's the most imposing part of the airport. Drab, and weary, and noisily colonial. The stop-point for the colonial ancestors who came to these shores to die of fever for King, Queen and Country. There was a long wooden table which wore the stain marks of many spilled beers. Some aesthete of a customs boss had tried to liven the hall up with cheap tawdry armchairs that reflected an immutable destiny and lineage. The floor was of hard cement spotlessly clean but for a few scattered and hurriedly finished cigarettes and stray bits of paper ends torn off portmanteaux and suitcases at the arrival gate by the absent-minded and bored ground hostess with too much lipstick on her thick lips. Outside, the sun shone bitterly; a gay indolent wind was fluttering the frayed national flag for which we have not yet been called to die. The parking lot glistened with important limousines in between which a few dispirited urchins lurked in the hope of finding something to steal. In the hall, the lazy fans were blowing hot air, determined to offer the unwilling service into which they had been pressed years ago. Rust and age could not permit.

Amamu stood by the counter. He had gone through three beers as he chatted up a small fellow with horn-rimmed glasses about some forgotten lawsuit. A group of Lebanese merchants, apparently expecting an augmentation of their numbers, were trying to interest him in some deal involving imports/exports, the basis and the end of all businesses in Africa. His father-in-law was sipping brandy from a tall glass forced on him by his son-in-law.

The plane touched down at twelve noon. Two black Mercedes cars whizzed across the tarmac to collect two ministers who were returning from a conference in London organized by the World Committee for the Protection of African Interests, South of the Sahara.

The first busload rolled up to the arrival gate. Its content was largely Indian, Lebanese and European. They clutched their briefcases with fear, as they had been told to beware of pickpockets at every African airport.

The second bus rolled up. Amamu saw his wife sitting by the left side. The Johnson family, father, mother and a couple of old-maidenly women, had pushed their way through, bursting towards the little gate to reach the bus.

That place is beyond bounds. Can't you read? It was an orderly in white overalls, his face bathed in sweat and irritation. She came down, slowly, a little uncertain smile on her face. She was small, copper-coloured. She bore her petiteness with the assured elegance of someone – a retired judge's daughter – who had just come back from England. She wore a mauve dress cut rather low and a pair of expensive-looking shoes to match. Her face bore a certain distant animation, heightened by the whole business of arriving home after five years abroad. Soft brown eyes marked out by deep scars of eyebrow pencil. Her nose slightly squat fitting pertly over a rather wide mouth which bore marks of a faint moustache. As she smiled, a fine row of teeth shone white and incisive. In that smile was revealed the remainder of her animation. She would be a strong-willed woman, from whose head goats cannot eat leaves. And passionate. Her twenty-eight years were lost in a girlish carriage reminiscent of a long-ago childhood of parental love, indulgence, secret passion at girls' boardinghouses, and the ecstasy of forgotten romances in her bed-sitter in Kilburn and Swiss Cottage. But the teeth were pure and artificial, products of one of those little factories in Europe that specialize in articles that could be stuck into any receptacle on the human body.

Amamu dashed through the cluster of in-laws and hugged his darling wife. Not very demonstrative, it was surprising that he did it. But it was over quickly. His courage had come and gone with the last surge of alcoholic joy.

Sammy was checking her through customs. The big burly official looked at him for a split second.

Passport, he grunted.

Sammy pushed Alice's passport to him as politely as he could. The man checked through slowly and deliberately.

Health certificate.

Sammy pushed the yellow card at him. He studied it, pausing now and then to take a look at Sammy.

Who is this? he asked.

The name is written there, here, Sammy said without emotion.

Don't talk to me like that. You can go to England and come but don't talk to me like that.

Sammy decided to remain silent. After a while when the man glared like a blazing bush, he bent his face down on the paper.

The lady should be here herself. She has no yellow fever.

Sammy dashed through the hall to the bar. Amamu was draining a large brandy, as he said, to Alice's health and safe homecoming.

He marched into the customs a few minutes later.

What is this about yellow fever? The lady is my wife.

The man who was looking through the booklet ignored him. A senior-looking official had pushed his way through.

Eh, lawyer, what is it?

It's my wife, Mr Addo.

His wife has no yellow fever, sir, the officer who inspected the papers said.

Mr Hammond, I have told you that you must not be rude to people here, because you don't know who they are. Mr Doe, come and take over from Mr Hammond. Mr Hammond, you will please wait for me in my office.

He had said his piece. He turned round now to Amamu.

Oh, lawyer, don't worry, sir. I hope you won't take it seriously, sir. Where are your wife's things? Have they been inspected by customs? I shall handle them myself, sir, straightaway.

He had once seen his Principal Secretary and the lawyer drinking at the Avenida Hotel.

They moved out of the airport into the bright sharp afternoon at about three. Traffic was heavy. The drive was silent. Now and then Amamu would ask a question.

So how is Frank Annobi? Is he still living in Golders Green?

Yes, and is still as drunk as hell. He and Susie are going steady, Susie Bartels.

The exchanges came to an uneasy halt. They wound their way through to a halt at the Ring Road Circle. There was a holdup. A police motorcyclist whizzed past.

The President is passing from the Castle to his residence in Flagstaff House. About ten cars ahead was a municipal night soil truck carrying its load from the former European area of Ridge, now occupied by senior African government officials. Alice put a handkerchief on her nose. The smell rose in the wave of the heat, descending on them with a malevolence that was almost a joke. They sat in the car glum and choked by the smell of suburban shit.

The presidential motorcade passed. He sat at the back of the third Rolls-Royce, alone, looking out of his bullet-proof windshield on the world.

I bet he doesn't shit. It was Sammy; he had forgotten the lady's presence.

Amamu had paid the deposit on a three-bedroom estate house in Kaneshie, tucked away on a street without a name, like most streets in the city. He had been planting flowers. The result was a row of zinnias, yellow and laughing sunflowers encircled by milk-bush. Chairs had been arranged on the little grass for a celebration.

Yaro stood alert to welcome home his master's wife.

The first Saturday following Alice's homecoming, her husband called a party. It began as a lazy dull day promising rain, heat and short tempers. The heat hung over the earth like a sick man's blanket dampened by a long fever sweat playing heavily over the bare earth like old theatre curtains that no wind can sway. A few dark clouds straddled the sky's span playing tricks as they rushed to the seacoast and ran back over the city with silent laughter.

Amamu sat in the living room, not exactly sober, and not exactly drunk. Yaro came in reeking of his own sweat and muddy. He had been arranging his flower pots. His master had called him thrice.

Yes sah, masa.

You no finish for outside?

No sah.

Finish quick and come clean for inside. We get party tonight. Big people dey come. Clean for all de glass, plate, fork, spoon, knife everything. You hear?

Yes sah. Yaro shuffled off on silent feet. Amamu stretched himself in the armchair, covering his face with yesterday's *Daily Graphic*.

The sun set without the promised rain falling. The sky was brilliantly lit by the new moon, which had burst through the clouds and cleared the remnants of their pranks. There were quite a number of stars twinkling on Christmas cards in faraway lands in pale obeisance to the luminous assertion of their matron the moon.

On the steps stood Yaro clad in a spotless clean pair of white trousers on which a button was missing, and a white shirt, beaming benevolently, pleased with the promise of an easy evening of self-indulgence. His master had asked him to welcome the guests. He bore him a love like that of his own son, took care of him whenever he came home drunk.

Yaro came from the north. A sharp lean character who said he left his white master because he wanted to turn him into a woman. He came from a village a few miles from Tumu near the border with Upper Volta where he said guinea fowls sold threepence apiece. He was part of a large family of thirty-five children who lived in their mothers' huts. His mother was the fourth of seven wives. They grew their millet and harvested it, shared the bush fowls and waited for the yearly rain to come. Some of his elder brothers had married and moved to their own compounds with their newly wed wives who cried as they were led from their fathers' homes away to their husbands' homes. His sisters were taken away into marriage by tall suitors who came on gay horses from neighbouring villages. They spoke with the elders, and after long palavers, they brought cattle and sheep and took the crying girls away. Gradually the household broke up. He and a few others were left to till the brown unyielding earth to bring home at harvest time just enough to feed their aging father, the women and the children, who, as Allah willed it, were still being born.

Then there came a terrible year. Famine hit the land full in the face in a sharp angry manner. Before it, locusts had come one day from the east devouring the millet fields in a swift swoop and vanishing towards Mecca. Everyone said Allah was angry with his children. The fields were brown, the millet reeds stood in their melancholy loneliness swaying in the harmattan wind, shorn of every grain of corn. Farmers hung their hoes on their shoulders and watched openmouthed. The imam called a great prayer meeting at which the Holy Book was read and Allah was begged by two hundred voices in the falling mosque.

He went to the prayer meeting with his father, as the oldest of the remaining children carrying his father's sheepskin. The elders crouched on the ground and counted their beads as the imam read from the Holy Book. That night, he decided to run away. Some of the boys in his age group who had left home returned at Ramadan with shirts and Mama with whom he was circumcised brought a bicycle.

The prayer meeting ended just when the new moon was peering over the baobab behind the mosque. He didn't sleep very well that night. He had tied his belongings into a bundle. His grey festival smock and a pair of new sandals, and a short farming smock. At the first cock he said his prayers to Allah and slipped out of his mother's hut. The journey to Kumasi was long and dusty. He arrived on the third day hungry. As he leaned against a shed near the Kejetia market, Allah intervened. He saw Seidu. Seidu was boy for a white man who built roads. He had a nice room with two European chairs and a water cooler. The next morning Seidu took him to the army barracks and pointed out a shed and said, There, it is there they sign for soldier. He wore an old pair of Seidu's trousers and a brown shirt. On his feet were his new pair of sandals. More people came. A man from his own home – he had been missing long ago since he was a mere boy – dressed in clean khaki of the army appeared. He had two ropes on his shoulders and everyone called him 'Couple'.

Fall in straight line, he barked. Allah dey. Those who had bad foot were asked to step out. His clothes were clean. Allah dey, true. Sule came to his position in the line, and he did not speak the white man's language to him. He spoke the language of his home town. Allah dey.

First he was assigned as an orderly to an officer. He worked for him for two years. Then the war ended. Allah is good. He got a gratuity of £18 13s. 4d.

Alice was dressed in a beautifully designed cloth with patterns of dancing butterflies. The kaba shirt was cut low around the neck. The V shape revealed a pair of honey-coloured breasts pushed up in arrogance by a steady brassiere. Her hair was done into a dome, curled at the front and the rest held by a glinting silver bracelet. She held in her tiny hand a little wineglass which she twirled round in blissful remembrance of a faraway land and another joyous occasion.

Amamu walked out trying desperately to look sober. Sammy, keep an eye on Yaro if the booze is to last the whole night.

Yaro is a Moslem, he doesn't drink, Sammy said.

Ask him if I didn't catch him two weeks ago carrying away a half-empty bottle of scotch.

Yaro stood there smiling at the good humour of his master.

The guests began to arrive. The first was Francis Addison, who worked for the Academy of Sciences. He was the Director of the Institute of Standardization. He was a tall half-caste arrogant man whose mother, it was whispered, was a notorious Sekondi prostitute who slept with a rich garlic-soaked Syrian soap maker and missed her period as a result and bore him a son. The boy preferred to use his mother's maiden name, which sounded better than Feisal. He had a glittering career at M.I.T. from where he walked straight into the Director of Standardization's chair in the newly established Academy. His field was civil engineering. He was still a gay bachelor, though girls whispered that his penis was very very weak. He was fond of asking people for spare French letters. He came into the door with his swagger and a cigarette holder.

After him came a crowd. Among them was Donald Ashittey, the D.P.P.; open-minded bon vivant who had a reputation for wit and incisive sarcasm both in and out of court. Close after him was Susana Manley, five times married. She was aging but refused to recognize the fact. She had the reputation of raping young boys with salacious zeal. A nineteen-year-old junior clerk in the Ministry of Fuel and Power was her latest passion. Then there were two women, friends of Alice, who on entering promptly seized the chairs in the right-hand corner of the room and talked about London the whole evening.

Yaro had started serving drinks. Conversation limped precariously from one subject to another without focus.

So how's the courts? It was Francis Addison talking across the room to the D.P.P.

Fine. Knee deep in work. Clearing a lot of work before the legal vacation. And how's the Academy, and Standardization? By the way, what exactly do you people do?

At this a few people giggled. The Director of Standardization was not amused. Not in the least.

Well, if you want to know, we check on the standards of all new products entering the market. New companies are coming into the country. We must make sure that their products are up to the standard. We check on plastic products, cotton and clothing, all appliances – electric irons, stoves. With that, Mr Addison, B.A., M.A., from M.I.T. kept mute, his eyes challenging the whole gathering. The D.P.P. was not intimidated.

Then what about those electric stoves which are exploding and killing people at Akosombo and Tema? Were they not standardized? You instead of those impregilo mechanics must be prosecuted in court. This brought the place down. The laughter was still going when Paul Dunyo entered. Paul was the editor of the *Daily Clarion*, a noisy rag of dubious politics. He had the reputation of an ass, but believed in his own wisdom, and readily got brilliant about every subject under the sun. He was about four-eleven, and his enemies put him at three feet ten and assigned him a wandering pigmy ancestor.

Eh, what are you people so gay about? he asked, a ready smile on his face.

Your height, said the D.P.P.

But I am taller than Napoleon. At this even the two spinsters in the corner burst into laughter.

Drinks flowed freely. Amamu was the perfect host, half drunk. Alice sat on the sofa with her friends from London and talked about London and some of the latest scandals among the African students.

Let's have some high life, high life. Donald got up on his feet and had squatted in front of the radiogram.

Soon everyone was dancing the high life. Except Paul Dunyo, who kept his seat, clutching in his tiny hand a half-empty glass of beer. Amamu danced in a middle-aged kind of way with his demure wife flashing her artificial teeth with joy.

A cool night outside, still. A few stray dogs were sleeping on the asphalt street, hugging the warmth into their empty stomachs. A spirit of silence was abroad. Cars dashed past screeching their tyres on the curb and hurrying their contents towards some seedy nocturnal rendezvous north of the city.

About midnight Colonel Letsu came in. A fair-coloured man in his mid-thirties. He rose from the ranks after the rigours of a spell in Mons and Aldershot. A born snob without the knowledge of what exactly to be snobbish about, he carried his five foot seven like a colossus, impatient with 'civilians' and obsequious to his superiors. This had earned him a quick rise. He had acquired alongside his rapid rise a new language which was neither English nor his native tongue. He spoke the two with the same accent. He had driven to the party in his new Mercedes 250 just delivered from Germany. His name was engraved on the dashboard. He was held in great esteem by both his friends and his enemies, all of whom granted him ability. He was a vindictive man, a snob who once knew poverty and was now determined to cover up his path with the roar and thunder of his martial office.

Yaro approached him, cut him a sharp salute and said, Masa, what you go drink?

Champagne! This calls for champagne. There was no champagne so the Colonel settled for brandy and ginger. Paul Dunyo had got up and stood offering his seat to the Colonel, who looked at him and with a sneer said, Thank you, editor, how are you? and sat down while the editor moved away nervously looking for somewhere else to stand without offending the Colonel.

Susana Manley had got up. She had moved across the room to the Colonel.

Dance, please. He pretended not to have heard.

Oh, Colonel, excuse me, dance, please.

The Colonel would not budge. He was tired, he said, he didn't feel like a dance, he would leave very soon.

Susie – she still carried the scars of a disastrous love affair with the Colonel (when he was a Captain, three years ago) – tried hard now, aware that everyone was looking, to pull the Colonel out of his chair first gently and then hard. The Colonel let go of her hand. Susie landed on her backside, knocking down Yaro with a tray of glasses trying to meander his way among the guests. Susie was drunk. She had danced with no one except with Paul Dunyo, who had hectored her into a clumsy dance – a cross between a bear hug and a series of hops.

Yaro stood his ground firmly. The glasses flew in several directions, smashing against the front wall and splintering on the floor. One of the old spinsters in the corner shouted, Hurrah. Everyone ignored her call to cheer broken glasses, a custom fervently adhered to among Africans. Susie was still on the floor. A pained look on her face, her eyes cold staring at the Colonel. The room was silent now, and no one knew what to say. The gentlemen wondered whether they should go to the unfortunate lady's aid, or turn their faces away or start a new irrelevant conversation. Before they knew what it was Susie had thrown one of the half-broken glasses at the Colonel. It caught him straight on his nose with a tinkling explosion. The Colonel, the soldier that he was, was not battle ready. He was caught off guard by a determined adversary whose weapons were lethal if slightly unconventional. A string of invectives hit the roof, as their source marched in a swift formation on the enemy, who had not yet recovered from the shock of a surprise attack. No one knew where he came from. Paul Dunyo had thrown himself in a swift dash at the woman. He was holding on to her buttocks. An arc movement from the woman's arm sent the editor flying towards the spinsters in the corner, who before their visitor arrived were screaming, Mewuo, mewuo, which is Fanti for I am dying, I am dying. Donald had in a flash placed himself between the woman and her target; he had got hold of her two arms in mid-air in an aim for the kill at the infantry commander who was mentioned in dispatches for bravery and gallantry in the Congo. Meanwhile, Paul Dunyo, turning a falling ground into a sleeping place, was still sprawling on top of the women, who were now crying, Jesus, Jesus, Mr Dunyo, you are hurting our thighs, please, Mr Dunyo, you are hurting us.

Swine, swine, swine, I say; pr pr pr.r.r.r. Yes, look at me, look at me very well, you son of a bitch from the bush. The woman was raging and rearing like a harmattan storm. The infantry commander, overcome by the swift progress of events and the unexpected velocity of the abuses – both in depth and loudness, sat quietly resigned staring in vacant surprise at the woman who was once his lover. Everyone was on his or her feet. Amamu was the only one who sat listening to his wife whimpering:

Please, Donald, take her away. What is this, eh? What is this?

Donald took Susie's arm. He was leading her away. He was pleading with her. But her fury was not yet spent. She hurled every abuse, every invective at the Colonel, gave intimate details of his ancestry and of his personal hygiene. She had allowed herself to be led into the yard now. Her voice rose in the night air like the call to prayer at the mosque.

What kind of Colonel? Eh, what kind? With this she attempted to break loose again. Donald held on to her with the determination of a desperate beggar.

Without warning, Susie burst into tears. Hysterical sobbing tears. She was not crying because of the indignity she suffered at the hands of someone whose bed she had once shared. She was crying for her life: at forty the magic of a glamourous youth, of lovers, of heady perfumes, of trips to Lome, Takoradi, Kumasi, and dances at residences – officials' homes – was ended. She had known many lovers since seventeen. Her father was a wealthy timber merchant who earthed up on the west coast in the late nineteenth century. He was reported to have come from Trinidad, some claimed he was a Brazilian. Those were the days when young ex-slaves made the return trip home to their ancestral lands. Mr Stephen Manley was among them. He worked hard for the firm of F. Swaniker. Around 1930, during the great depression, the firm sold the business to the ambitious fifty-year-old Mr Manley, and fled the continent of fever and instant death. He was home. There were no more journeys before him. He had married a local woman from Dixcove among the Ahanta people. Business picked up again. He turned to timber, at that time a new commodity that was greatly in need by a deforested Europe. He made a sizable fortune. Susie was his favourite daughter. At twelve, she had begun to take care of her brothers and sisters. Their mother had died suddenly of some dreadful unnameable African disease. The following year, old Manley sent her to Holy Child, a good solid Roman Catholic secondary school in Cape Coast. Manley died in 1947 at sixty-seven. His bones were laid among his ancestors. He left behind a good fortune: six houses, and a flourishing business. His eldest son, Alexander Clifford Manley, was the turning point in the family's destiny. His father had sent him to England when he was barely nine years old. He went to a private school in Surrey, and had an athletic career at Harrow. He proceeded to Oxford. There, according to his sister, he fell among criminals, who turned him into a homosexual, and when after two years he was sent down, he took a room in Kensington. There he drank his fortune with a band of loud-mouthed Jamaicans who had come over on the banana boats. When he heard the old man had passed away, he flew home and sold the business to a pock-marked Lebanese merchant who made caustic soda soap near Sekondi market. After a week, he flew back to gay London with enough money, which made a good deal of difference to the postwar austerity of that ancient city. With seventy thousand pounds in his pocket, he bought a twelve-room house in Ealing, a restaurant, and a series of women. He died six years later, they say, of tuberculosis. In death, he was declared bankrupt.

Susie managed to exist. She was redeemed by one of her father's old friends, a Mr Thompson of an old Elmina family. He married her. Mr Thompson was near sixty-eight and Susie was sixteen. He spoiled her in memory of his friend, old Manley. She saw the gay life of Accra and liked it. After salting away enough of Thompson's money, she fled the marital home with a notorious philanderer called Bobo de Boy from Sekondi.

Now they led her away howling, pouring her woes into a bout of tears that streamed down her once beautiful face. Here was the sorrow that was born in the memory of a past which could have been better, the sorrow for a future, now, that would have been different.

The fight was the lever to a gloomy rest of the night. Try as they could, the evening was ruined. The Colonel sat glum. Paul Dunyo, after six beers, was making a pathetic attempt to dance with one of the old maids. After a while the Colonel excused himself and drove into the deep night. Amamu still sat at the table steadily finishing a bottle of scotch and lowly tuning 'When I Survey the Wondrous Cross'. Alice had retired into her room. A few latecomers with two girls with faces like crocodiles had attacked the remainder of a bottle of brandy and were dancing noisily.

Go home, everyone, come on, go home. It's over. It was Amamu. He had got up. The dancers paused. They were looking at him. I say, go home! Quickly they grabbed their women in disbelief. Yaro stood at attention on the first step and muttered:

Good night, masa, good night.

## ••• Chapter 10a

London. Wet morning. Defecation of dogs on the pavement. The counterblast is fired from the ships in the misty harbour; there is a crowd rushing around Hyde Park singing obscene songs, the wheels of an old coach came off in the shadow of the Marble Arch, a crowd has gathered. Our dog days are washed clean by the intense focus of the artificial spark from lit fires of suburban homes, where on the corner the old friendly Jewish shopkeeper who does business with blacks is flashing his teeth after a kosher meal – a few of the blacks ran away with his money, but it is no matter, Jews and blacks must stick together.

One wet Sunday at Speakers' Corner, the one-eyed Negro from Jamaica talked about Rhodesia and South Africa. It was the week the slogans went up on walls, and black heads were busted in Notting Hill Gate. Send the wogs home. Alex and I rushed across Battersea Park looking desperately for a pub. Then I must return to my loved one, my new bourgeois love from my native land. We were whispering about marriage in those sad days of dog shit on pavements.

Please consecrate and approve our bodies, as feasts for your never satisfied appetite, that it be acceptable for us. Take and eat of this

For this is my body,

my body I offer, my blood I offer, a sacrament.

That summer of romance, of inane promises, of delusions of love's redemption in the bed-sitter near Kilburn when we drowned our uncertainties in gallons of pale ale, broke and renewed faith in extravagant oaths and testimonies of our fidelity.

Diminishing afternoon in the darkness of afterlove a cruel mocking laughter strangles the only joy left. I have carefully prepared the event, like Pope John, my bags are packed to trek across the vineyard of my father's, sit beneath his seventeenth-century thatched cottage heavy green with weeping willows. For word has come that Okigbo the elephant has walked to hell.

Then I turned to the Poet, and he said: Let him be first with thee now and me second.

Here, in the age of bombs and the perfection of political stratagems, a host shall flee their homeland, and lap up the paradise of exile lands. Old men shall die in transit between little arguments produced by trained soldiers from Sandhurst. A thousand raindrops shall dance in the fertile womb of time. Graves shall remain unmarked for who will want to read the tombstones of malefactors rotting in the hot African sun in the green field by the ocean near the army barracks.

Across the mighty bridge a host has gathered in lamentation for Okigbo the elephant is dead. It is no matter. The last patrol shall return at dawn and announce the arrival of the former rulers. And a mining village shall name a street after a former Colonial Secretary. The ancient termagant shall tell tales of ancient heroes of mighty Africa, of Chaka, of the conquering clansman of the legendary Soundiata the prince of the Malinke. Old scrolls shall be read in gilded halls proclaiming the glory of Koumbi Saleh, the wisdom of the scholars of Sankure, of mighty African rulers who bargained their subjects for heads of tobacco, kegs of gunpowder and a few yards of cloth that could scarcely cover the nakedness of their wives.

In the banquet hall of a famous Swedish publisher one grim winter in Stockholm the hostess demure and comely graceful and stately all nose said, Let the Africans climb the table against the wall and say their names aloud whence they came what words did they have for their Scandinavian brothers and sisters. The Algerian stood in the corner and made an impassioned speech about the land of a million martyrs, the flow of Algerian blood that nurtures the fires of the revolution. Vive la révolution.

This green voluptuous seasmell of London's pubs proclaims a mystery which Roger and I, demons in the March showers of an English spring, can in no way understand for this earth proclaims its own truth: my Scandinavian, my English brothers that a virtue shall elude mankind in spite of a million paschal lambs slaughtered and offered to greedy gods who will continue to doze in this millennium.

The kneading of the clay is the most important task that we face, for the builder demands the responsibility to build new bodies in his image. The dinosaurs have returned to earth, see,

see them warbling through the centuries. They are holding a banquet in the halls of the renaissance men, balded by aeons of waiting.

What has Africa to contribute to the world? asked the learned professor.

If you have no history create one, if you have no culture, invent one, for the question is being asked, and, brother, you must come forth with an answer, pronto.

She fell madly in love with a Swiss gentleman. Secretly she wanted a mulatto baby, fair with long hair. When the man left for Europe she pursued him. Two years after she came home with a fair baby girl with long hair. The species must be improved. They have stayed black for too long, and black is not beautiful. Her mother and her aunts in Cape Coast screamed over the baby, What a beautiful baby, and named her She Who Was Born in the White Man's Country.

In Stockholm the African students held a soiree all in three piece speaking Swedish fluently. Long Live Africa and her Presidents. An African leader will be addressing his subjects in St Pancras Town Hall tonight.

The world will be emptied of matter, a prognostication shall be offered by hoary-headed elders under nim trees pipes in their mouths lamenting the many unmentionable sins committed by present-day youth against tradition. The classical gentleman, well read in Herodotus at Cambridge, shall solve the educational problems of Africa by a document that must have its preamble in Latin, and be larded with quotations from Heraclitus.

For childhood shall end here upon these ecstatic shores where a renewal of faith shall be achieved by the sacrificing of our manhood's innocence, for as the Leader said, we, the Africans, must be jet propelled into the twentieth century.

For this earth, my brother, shall claim you for her own. The boys come one day shouting on the pavement, Come out, you son of a gun, we are on our way to Oxford. Kodzo was among them tall and silent. We trooped down to Paddington and caught the one forty-five. I nearly sat on a pale girl's bag. When I lifted it up she snatched it, and a venomous blond man stared waiting for a fight. Dirty wogs, why don't you go home to your own countries? Joe was about to deliver a lecture about our British heritage how our wealth – both material and human –

built London, profits from our gold, diamonds, cocoa – of which 230 million was given us at independence – and the human trade raised the tall sooty buildings of the City with its bowler-hatted gentlemen – but poor Joe he didn't make it. Instead he went to Kenya to take a job with UNESCO, to teach English as a second language. We left Neville behind, eloquently finishing off the last of a series of Teachers in the garden – it wasn't much of a garden – with apple trees leafing in the early spring sun. Teach the kids cricket, it's a damn good game for revolutionaries. Karl Radek will prefer poetry plus suicide. The train swept through the greening countryside of England, once our mother country. We were silent for a distance, the hay preparing for the sun that comes but rarely in a land, as Kodzo said, of freaks. For we, the best of nature's freaks, African intellectuals, are returning from Oxford where there still is a watering place by the name of a pub and we drowned our exile tears in gallons of good English beer.

For we, my brother, were growing on that train, nearer death. Robert, my landlord from Kingston, Jamaica, was an amiable man with two lovely children and a wife who rarely frowned. When the police rang my doorbell, Robert would answer the door and tell them, Go away, you rass cloths. He was a good solid man who still dreamed of his island in the sun with calypsos and poinsettias blooming at doorways where rent is low and good country air is available by the stream for all to breathe. Aren't we all dreaming of our native land in this great city once more on the breast of women in negligees, snoring in patriotic rhythm our national anthems and waving our miniature national flags at shit trucks roaring away in dark tropical evenings when moons are tired? Aren't we all, my brother?

In Stanleyville, the simbas raped a whole nunnery and killed an Alsatian dog. A Sunday paper carried the picture of the dying dog under the headline

African Savagery Resurgent

They are plotting the killing of one tribe in Britain's model of democracy. The reason is that they are too arrogant. The young General will be accountable to God alone. Long Live British Parliamentary Democracy.

Some African dignitaries were walking around the gates of

Buckingham Palace wearing amulets and talismans, and some were chewing rare African timber. So I fell into a long conversation with the woman near me. Her brother is in Chad, she herself is French, she married an Englishman, could I take a parcel for her brother in Chad when I was going back to Africa. In the little village outside Warsaw, some Africans were seen at a Chopin recital. Do you know Chopin's work? Do Africans play Chopin? In my desperation I joined the group going to Oxford to hear Neville talking revolutionary talk.

Word came that our totems had collapsed while we were away. Here we are drinking March in a glass of Teachers while our totems fall. Okigbo's totem was the elephant. Mine was the hippopotamus of the Volta River. Kodzo's was the cockroach. In my room we talked about the changes that must come, that Africa needs a spiritual, psychological, mental revolution. Look at African education. Look at the corruption of our politicians, look at the moral decay that has engulfed our beloved homelands. Yes, Africa needs a revolution. Long Live Africa. Then we went our several ways, some to sleep with our wives, others to fornicate with willingly lonely spinsters in one-room apartments in Golders Green. Tomorrow too we shall meet and discuss the revolution that Africa needs. There can be only one revolution. The permanent revolution. So said the Gambian Trotskyite who fled from Moscow when the Soviets were beating Africans up in Sochi and Tashkent. And they say they have no colour bar. Hypocrites. All Communists are hypocrites, just like the capitalist hyenas! Long Live Africa.

God gave the black man nothing but dreams. He is a fantastic dreamer upon little matters. Above all he is a lazy sonofabitch! Give him an inch and he will be uppity and demanding equal rights and equal pay. So they were saying when Hannibal crossed the Alps with his elephants. But they work hard if you are there to supervise them. Ask the twentieth-century saint Schweitzer, who gave his life to Africa. Besides the fellows are ungrateful. Look at all that we did for them. Brought them civilization, forced them out of their filthy animal skins, and put decent clothes on them, and above all, above all else, taught them the English language. Get out of Africa? They will reverse into barbarism. You watch. Africans will pee anywhere, the bastards, we can't stand them, can we? And they smell like hell.

In that hour of my animal resistance of death, give me strength that I may endure the charity of my pallbearers after my mouth is closed. For in the evening, let it all be over; spare me the kindness of the earth and the gentility of the vulture, veil away from me your understandable love, and fashion out of this universal hate that gnaws my insides a flaming sword of vengeance.

Our Father Who art in heaven, do whatever pleases you. For ours is only this terrible penalty.

A band from home is playing in Trafalgar Square. It is playing African airs on European instruments; a young African singer is imitating Sammy Cooke in the shadow of Nelson's Column. They came from villages in dark Africa to sing to the English capital city, to sing to ears fed on Mozart and Schubert; but for the junkies and the vagabonds of the city, they would have had no audience. A man stood by in tatters, a month's beard grizzling on his face. Chewing the cud he spat on a pigeon dropping, turned away and gave his immutable verdict:

Send the wogs home.

His rags fluttering in the gay May wind he wound his way towards his underground home.

## ••• *Chapter 11*

Friday afternoons were set aside. They were set aside by the school authorities. These were the afternoons on which the children marched to a whistle to the cemetery. There they spent the time cleaning up the whole burial ground, sweeping in between the graves, collecting and burning dried-up flowers from new graves and making a bonfire under the coconut tree on the left corner.

The cemetery was not very large. People said they had buried people on top of other people. Gravediggers making new graves would dig up the bones of someone's beloved husband, brother, sister, father or mother who departed to the Lord in the year So-So and So and was resting in peace till the resurrection day.

When a teacher went with them, the children worked briskly and hard. When they went by themselves under the direction of the class prefect, who was one of them, they worked a little and played a lot. They spent the time reading the writings on the tombstones, especially the missionary section where the first missionaries from Bremen were buried. They gave their lives to Africa, in the service of God, to save the heathens from eternal damnation. There were strong German names which they couldn't pronounce. But they spelled them out. One boy who said his father was a German scholar said it for them. There was one particular grave they loved. Its gravestone was made of shiny black marble, with beautiful old German letters carved on it. Then there were chains which, as it were, were intended to hold the main slab down. The boys knew the story of those shiny iron chains. The man in the grave was said to be a lodge member, a kind of spiritualist. When he died around 1930, he was buried the same day according to the rules of his lodge. He was a tall strong man who rode a horse through town. He was not exactly a missionary but had something to do with the mission. He smoked a kind of cigar which they said was as long as his nose. Its smell was strong and pungent. The first day they buried him, the people who lived around the cemetery said they smelled his cigar – in the night always on the stroke of twelve. Then they heard the clatter of a horse's hoofs on the street for one hour. It came down from the south end and paused near the first cemetery gate, and went back clack-ko clack-ko down the road and back. This was heard for one hour every night from midnight, those who lived near the cemetery said. Those who were strong came out, but fled for they saw Johan Wiegrabbe on his horse. He sparkled in a silvery fire, and his cigar glowed in his burning mouth. Many people heard about it. A complaint was lodged with the Church authorities. One man, an old man, volunteered to challenge the ghost. They saw him the next morning near the western gate dead, a thin foam at the side of his mouth. His head was bashed in, they say, by the horse's hoofs. The spiritualists were called in. After a long preparation, they put a chain on the ghost. The chain, they said, was forged by Rosicrucians in a town in Bavaria where the cult is powerful. Since then, Johan had never been seen or heard riding his horse.

This Friday they had marched into the cemetery under the whistle of the class prefect. Their teacher could not come. The line broke up immediately they entered the cemetery; they scattered among the graves, some throwing off their shirts, others making for the first shade under the coconut trees. Three of the boys had wandered off to the far end. They cleared a stack of debris, dead leaves of the forget-me-not, and sat down.

I don't want to die. It was a statement. After a short pause, they picked up the subject.

But everybody will die.

The way they are inventing things now, by the time we are grownups they will invent a medicine against death.

Silly. If no one dies, there will be too many people in the world.

What is wrong with too many people?

Imagine that all the people who are dead get up, there will be no place to put your foot.

That's true. But that is how it will be on Judgement Day. Everyone who has lived on the earth as far back as Adam and Eve will wake up for judgement.

Yes. What about those buried upon others? Some of the bones are mixed up. Then what about those who are drowned, and their bodies eaten by sharks and they were never found? Then all those who died on the battlefield.

I don't want to die.

Have you ever seen somebody die before?

Yes; my cousin. The daughter of my mother's sister. Her mother died. So she came to stay with us. One day she died. They all became silent now, as they huddled together close to the boy who was narrating the story.

Tell us. How did she die?

Oh, she just died one day. She said she was feeling pains in the stomach; my mother gave her some purgative. Then for a while she was all right. But in the night she was screaming, saying something was eating her intestines. She started to talk wildly saying she saw a woman who had come there. Several women. They were sitting there, and with long sticks they were pulling at her intestines, they were eating them, they were now going for the heart. She screamed and screamed. That night my mother hired a truck and we took her home to our village. She screamed half the way, as my mother cried and cried, and begged her not to die. I also begged her not to die. We arrived in our home town at dead of night. They put her on a bed. A medicine man, he was one of our uncles, came; he burned leaves and prepared herbs. But at dawn she died, very quietly she died.

Then she died? asked one person.

Yes.

That day people came. They took her to the bathhouse and bathed her. They made a bed in the anteroom and laid her on it. She was there all day. I went to sleep in the room next to her because there was no other room.

Were you not afraid?

No, I was not afraid.

Did you cry?

Silly, a man doesn't cry. It is only women who cry.

So what happened?

People came, more people. Then the agbadza boys brought their drums. My uncle had bought them a tin of akpeteshie. They drummed all day. They fired some muskets, aprim muskets, the big ones that make a powerful noise far away. They say it is to call the spirit of the dead person when they fire them. In the afternoon, my grandmother, my mother and some other women left with a song through the lanes of the village. They called my cousin's name near every bush, behind every grove. They were weeping, weeping and sweating. I wanted to follow them but my mother said: Go home. Children don't come along to search for a spirit. I stood outside and heard them wailing through town. They returned some hours later singing a dirge about an only child, an orphan who has died. She was an orphan. Her mother had died. Her father was a goldsmith who had fled up country because of debt. No one heard of him.

Did you go to the burial?

Yes. Two people carried her on their heads. She must be heavy. But she was only a little girl. They say people become very heavy when they die. They roamed the lanes with her, sometimes on the run with the dead body, sometimes slowly. The agbadza boys continued drumming. The women were singing the song about an orphan lost at the estuary. We arrived at the banigla about sunset. The carriers were tired. Then they put her down beside a newly dug grave. The women started a fresh bout of weeping. I nearly wept too. But I remembered a man is not supposed to weep. He weeps in his head. Then my uncle the medicine man poured libation. I didn't hear much of what he said. But he said if she was killed by people, she should seek vengeance. And quickly too. Then he gave her into the hands of the elders, those who had gone ahead into the land of spirits. Then they put her in the ground, and covered her with earth. The women burst into weeping again, calling her name, calling her name in song.

They didn't sing any hymns?

No. She was not baptized.

Then she will not go to heaven.

She will go to purgatory, where she will be washed of her sins.

Eh?

It is so. That night the agbadza boys drummed till the next day. They never seemed to tire. People danced, and some even made jokes about things and spoke lightheartedly and consumed glasses upon glasses of akpeteshie.

How long ago now?

Let me see. '45, '46, '47; three years.

Do you think she has rotted and become bones?

I think perhaps. Maybe.

If you see the bones, you can't recognize and say it is her.

Perhaps.

When on Judgement Day how are all those bones going to wake up?

They will be given new bodies by God. At least those who sleep in the Lord.

What does that mean?

Those who were Christians and led Christian lives are supposed to sleep in the Lord.

A shout was raised from the entrance. Two of the boys were locked in a fight. It was Tokpo, who was trying to cheat the new boy from Hagbanu at the game of spinning snail shells. The boy had put sand in his eyes and had thrown him on the ground. The others rushed and lifted him. Tokpo was panting trying to remove the sand from his eyes, muttering something about going to teach the boy a lesson. Then somebody shouted from the gate that he thought he had seen the teacher's bicycle in front of the tailor's shop two houses away. Soon, they had grabbed their brooms, some cutlasses, and were working furiously. After about an hour, somebody suggested they go and have a look at the bicycle. One boy went near it. It was a Raleigh bicycle. Their teacher had a Hercules. Everybody abused the boy who raised the false alarm; the shape of his head was what they liked abusing. It was like a kerosene tin because it had corners. Some smart mathematicians said it was a trapezium, some said it was a rectangle. One very imaginative boy said with grim finality that it was like a war boat. Everyone agreed with a yell, and laughter. Time to go however. They sorted out the shirts and vanished into the fast fading twilight.

## ••• *Chapter 11a*

This frame, smashed against such deadly countenances chained to the final idea of the death and decay of this body.

It is the only avenue of salvation, in this angered mood, self-denial, self-effacement become twin weapons to be worn into an equal and equally inconsequential battle. Hear their battle cry, my brother. A dog is delivering puppies in public. For you and me and all, a gathering must be proclaimed at our sacred grove, our worship must be renewed.

In the school chapel the art instructor shall fart like a dog. We will raise a hymn to drown the sound and the fury

The day Thou gavest, Lord, is ended

and march to the house beside the bakery where a lewd little girl lifts up her skirts and boys take a look for a shilling.

Then it would be all so very proper and right that one should die so that the rest shall be saved.

A siren is sounding in the streets this dawn proclaiming a new dispensation. The drum beat, slow and interspaced by yells, is summoning the rest of those washed ashore.

A prostitute brought the village pig butcher to the police station for giving her a counterfeit sixpence. The sergeant looked up and down and declared: It is a foolish case.

A very foolish case indeed.

Neville shall continue his hymns to a lynching and wonder forever whether Sibura will dance again in our time. For he saw Sibura dancing among the lilies beneath the hills of spice.

A screeching owl perched on the tree behind the house of illness. The coven of local witches is in session. We shall watch them helplessly from our homesteads strengthened by the herbalist's medicinal roots dug at dawn near the forked road leading to Ghost's Head. As our totems fall in the night caught on avia leaves in the shadow of the orange sun we shall watch them.

I am the created on God's Sixth Day in His immutable image

He made me so that I can come and serve Him in heaven. Those were the words of the catechism.

> Propitus esto. Domine, peccatis nostris, ne
> quando dicant gentes: Ubi est Deus eorum?

Who can say our turn has come to do this dance which is a matter for the hips, the hips?

My refusal to be drawn was interpreted as a primary act of rebellion against the established order of things. I am positive that I have erred somewhere along the line, and dear Lord, I am prepared to pay the price. Those who've never erred, those who've never even believed in the regime yet swaggered around in its shadow will proclaim the truth of what went wrong. Even the great academics will say who said what about the death of the General, to be transmitted by illiterate bank managers whose distant relatives are in the government. That is how it has become.

It is evident that roads and vehicular transport must not be introduced into the Gold Coast, for the Gold Coast African walks in Indian files, and he may be killed on these roads. Until he is taught not to walk in single file, it will be advisable that His Majesty's Government desists from building roads and importing vehicles into the colony. Besides it will be important to teach those who are attending the institutions of higher learning to think in English.

At the opening ceremony there was a good number of European-clad Africans – doctors, lawyers, traders, priests – who had awaited the fulfilment of their dreams.

The menagerie he built was burst into by soldiers who killed the deer, the ducks, the zebras and feasted all night. The lions and the tigers they couldn't touch.

An imposing array of native chiefs, dignitaries and their retinue of drummers and horn blowers assembled for the opening ceremony. Even *they* showed on their faces the receptive signs of the millennium planned for them. That day the natives drummed themselves into a state of utter exhaustion.

My death is remembered among these alien gravestones. For we, the children of Ashiagbor's house, went to hunt. When we returned our guns were pointing to the earth.

> I can stand everything – even though that horrible demon more dreadful than death, the being of terrors, even though madness were to hold up before my eyes the motley of the fool, and I understand by its look that it was I who must put it on, I am still able to save my soul.
>
> Kierkegaard

For the simple reason is that I am not. The more fool I. In the focal hour when the sounds coalesce, there will be offered a drink offering in the manner of hyssop and tears. And I will drink it. He hung upon a cross, my Lord, even He did not let the calabash pass.

So my woman of the sea was she that died in the death of my cousin when we were young in the butterfly fields in infant days years ago when my prisoner butterfly fluttered and fled away perhaps to the land of my forefathers.

Let the plucked rabbits (they are hens too) parade the streets with their dane guns. Death is an easier choice.

In my miracle fields, let them blossom like Mao's hundred flowers: their heads will be cut off.

The Cuban revolutionary came that year and addressed the comrades about the need for dying a little for mother Africa.

O motherland, we pledge to thee our death.

> If I have rightly understood thy words, replied the shade of that great soul, thy spirit is smitten with cowardice which many a time encumbers a man so that it turns him back from honourable enterprise, as a mistaken sight a shying beast. That I may deliver thee from this fear, I shall tell thee why I came and what I heard at the time when I first took pity on thee. I was among those who are in suspense, and a lady called me, so blessed and so fair that I begged her to command me. Her eyes shone brighter than the stars, and she began to speak to me with angelic voice in sweet, low tones.
>
> Dante's *Inferno*. Canto II

We used to limp into the convent, bruised sweaty urchins with running sores and noses. The sisters – demure Dutch maidens wrapped in yards and yards of white cloth, concealed in the innocence and overflow of white cloth – washed our sores with scissors and cotton dipped in pink smarting solutions. They smelled of faraway lands, and of potassium permanganate in yellow dust glistening on our sores. We were happy when they gave us sweets from Europe. We knew we were eating of the sweets of Europe. They themselves passed slowly like ghosts through their huge arbour planted with pawpaws, bananas, lilies, crocus, bougainvillea – and the eternal cemetery flower frangipani, the one we called the forget-me-not – in myriads of riotous colours when the rains are over in late May. Our running sores healed – sores heal quickly on young ones in Africa – we would return to supply the labour force in the convent garden of St Theresa with statues of saints placed in prominent field places. Our labour was construed as part of the Lord's work. The school bell ringing its funereal departure tone that school is over for the day is our signal to go through the convent gates meeting the Mother Superior with the greeting, Blessed be Christ, and she – a little figure with a face all wrapped up in white and wearing a cross bigger than Christ's when he laboured up the hill of Calvary – responded, And let his mercy endure forever, my children.

It was time to bring out our plantain fibre balls and kick them into the coming night in sweat and more bruises.

It was the year a man was caught exhuming a dead body at night. He was a medicine man who needed the jawbone of a dead magician in order to make more powerful medicines. He suffered from elephantiasis in one leg, and squinted so you didn't know whether he was looking at you or at a distant object.

He, like all of us, needed to make a new medicine. He himself died of a swelling disease through medicine placed on him by more powerful adversaries. He was buried at night by lantern light.

I gather the illusions of my beloved, the only gifts she left me as memories of those yellow days in sunflower fields when my prisoner butterfly flew away never to return.

Another like him flew through the green grass beside the sea where the rebel soldiers were shot one bright May morning. The report of Brens greeted the Atlantic surf echo with wild resoundings far far away towards the lighthouse and my Indian almond tree. Between their falling down – discreetly screened from public view by the soldiers – and the hysterical women screaming in all tongues of the land was revealed a singular apostrophe to my loneliness. All day, on the edge of the green field swarming with butterflies as the soldiery dismantled the tarpaulin tents, children and women of the land – including foreign correspondents – waded through the field looking for patches of execution blood. The sentence was passed in gilded halls where a red-eyed junior officer in battle array barked from an information desk to the crowd that had gathered to view the recalcitrant malcontents.

Then in May their blood watered the fields in payment of another bloodshed in the parched earth beneath the shadow of the Aviation Tower where birds build their nests all year refusing to emigrate to Europe. There was an empty gleaming sky through which gulls vaulted in measureless screeches of anguish, for the wind itself was still on this bright sharp morning of a shooting.

When the hunters return without game, they must go to bed without food. There is the decree.

Neville refused to leave his house upon the hill, and wrote more songs to the distant seasons of pimentos, and of screams on his small green hill, he and his dog, as the wind
sang in the yellow sunflower.

Those who transgressed against the laws of the clan in those days received either of two punishments: being sold into slavery, or execution. Those whose families had some money and standing escaped through the fire exit of the law into the distant lands of slavery on canefields. The poor went to their execution believing they were running an errand for the elders – errands in which goat-head is a terrifying symbol.

The ancestors – revered now for their infinite sagacity – decreed long ago that this land, this earth, my brother, shall witness a crashing collapse. And they drank brief drinks in toast to their wisdom in those days.

The song of the flower pickers purifies my flesh of desire I want to put my canoe on the river and go beyond. For our cliffs are our created tumults. The resounding hymns of a triumphant army let loose in the city streets.

The sore-covered little boy in the grip of a tropical disease known as yaws was brought into the convent one hazy morning when the rains were late. His eyes were large and grey, and his ribs were showing. The Mother Superior came shaking her head. His mother – a wide-faced woman with marks – answered the Reverend Mother's questions as truthfully as she could. Does he eat regularly? Yes, Sister. What food does he eat? Akasa and akple. No eggs? Eh, Sister, eggs? No! Of course natives have no understanding of nutritious food – so they feed their children on corn, and the poor dears end up with complicated cases of malnutrition further aggravated by terrifying native diseases.

The child with yaws died a week later. His people mourned for him, as appropriate for a child to be mourned – he was but four.

And on that magnificent continent, the diamond diggers and washers, the gold miners, the copper miners, the farmers on great European-organized plantations toil from sunrise to sundown so that their infants can die early of malnutrition. That is how it must be. Turn Africa into the central park of the world!

So my cousin love, she who came from the sea at the hour the moon slashes the sea in two beneath the shadow of my almond died, long long ago I cannot remember. As infants we run through the naked land naked near the barbed wire of the U.A.C. compound where the old storekeeper with a wheezing cough like a police whistle when smugglers are chased keeps the books in his neat cursive hand for his superiors to come and take stock of their holdings in those parts of Africa.

Into my gates I run searching for her at noon, for a restlessness has gripped me and this earth. I look for the curing wisdom herbs to burn on the altars of St Theresa when the sisters whisper the silent syllables of unheard prayers over infants that hastily close their eyes and die.

Lamb of God who taketh away the sin of the world, Pray for us. When she was gone, we gathered her beads in a pile and tied them into a neat bundle. Through the break in the reed fence made by greedy goats I believed she ducked and fled.

The eclipse of the sun came, a significant proclamation that all animals – especially domestic fowls that feed on dunghills – must retire for night has fallen upon the land where a bright sun should be shining. It was a pale, deathlike day on which the sun was caught by the futigive moon. Tins and cans were beaten along the lanes with cries: Please, moon, let the sun go for disaster will befall the land, dear moon, please let the sun go. Ancient poets made up recitations under the singular influence of homemade gin. For he who sings of the sun sings of life here in the land of death.

Sometimes she comes into my dreams, moon-faced, smiling, her coral teeth glistening in her dark round face. Then she will sit and talk for a long time. I will not understand a word she speaks. Suddenly as if in anger she will gather her tiny waist cloth and go away. It is always at that time that I will begin to fall fall from a great height, fall far far down. But I never reach the earth. Sometimes I will be in flight across the sky. I will fly in a blue heaven with clouds trailing my feet. We will career through the sky, like gulls over seas.

In the morning she will be gone. The bells will be ringing – the second bell – and my mother's oil lamp will be put out.

We sat and shared a drink once upon a time, and small talks about Africa for our thoughts lingered on departure; we dreamed of immense and fateful events that would turn our fortunes; we even dreamed of making money, buying luxury cars, and driving top speed through town. It was in those days that a local man who had made good in the city came home riding a brown horse. He was a stout majestic animal with wide nostrils, with the disconcerting habit of unfurling his penis at noon after his feed hour. His owner, a red-skinned gentleman who knew the world beyond our village, rode him through town on market days, paused now and then to exchange long traditional greetings with elders from the back of his horse. Everyone said how grand he looked on his horse. Everyone was very respectful to him because he was obviously a man of wealth and of foreign learning. But everyone said what a fool he was. Why didn't he buy a motor-car? Or even a bicycle. These may have little mechanical troubles now and then, but they go on for a long time. And with a motor-car he can make more money carrying people to market in our royal town. One day the beast died. We surrounded the brown beast in death foaming at the mouth. Its owner, the red-skinned man of wealth, swore a spell had been cast upon the beast by envious neighbours. He was going to Accra, and he would bring another beast more majestic and resplendent than the one that died. He vanished one day, in very mysterious circumstances. Seven months later they brought his body home for burial. He had died of a horse disease in the capital. We the children on the day of the horse's death were sad, for our hearts had lost one of their fervent delights. The owner we didn't care much for, even though we would have given our left arms to ride on the back of his brown Sudanese horse.

Long long after, when death came back again and took my brother, I remembered the horse, its nostrils aflame with a watery dignity, a defiant mien stamped on its forehead. Then the knowledge came home, that all that are noble must die; dogs, I forgot to tell you, barked at the horse and at the sun caught by the moon in the eclipse for they, the dogs I mean, were the only witnesses to the two acts.

She whom I loved went away to the other side of the season of grey dusks when winds from the north are high and dry and water is very cold. In my supreme innocence I wept for a miracle, for my goddess was dead and I could not believe in a death without signals.

Give us a sign, they said. The answer was that no sign should be given them save the sign of Jonah in the whale.

On my head was placed the long drum of the funeral, as the drums beat into my soul I heard her again calling over the waters calling from her primal bag and final tomb an old message in a youthful voice.

It was so very right that we should be the fashioners of our own scaffold, and our fingers should weave the final noose.

But we cannot, we must not, hang from cassava trees.

## ••• *Chapter 12*

Yaro! Yaro!

It was Alice calling Yaro. Yaro since the party last night had not turned up for work. Alice had stayed in her room all day. Now and then she screamed for Yaro in the hope that if he came he would fetch her a glass of iced water from the kitchen.

Amamu came home at lunchtime. Lunch had not been cooked. Alice was still in bed.

Yaro has not come to work, she said, as if addressing no one. Then she turned round and opened another page of *True Romance*.

Amamu stepped out into his car. Perhaps Yaro was ill. He had a vague recollection where he lived. He knew it was in Nima but the exact spot eluded him. But he would go and ask near the mosque. He remembered he dropped him home one night when it rained and stormed and a flood rose around the Circle – the one that has just changed names from Nkrumah to National Liberation.

Nima skirts the west central part of the city like a vulture. It was established during the Second World War when there was an American base in Cantonments. Squatters came and took land. A horde of camp followers, the inevitable community that grows around any army installation in poor underdeveloped or rather developing countries. Nima grew with the rapidity and alarm with which all slums grow. It was intended, in the minds of its inhabitants, to be a temporary dwelling place. They hoped to move when their fortunes changed for the better. But the war was over. The sojourners never moved. It always needs a Moses to move any captive race of squatters. Nima never had one. There was no chaste woman who could bring forth a Moses who would be placed in a basket for the Pharaoh's daughter to discover by the banks of a pleasant river full of joyous reeds. No river runs through Nima. Only a huge open gutter that stinks to heaven. The city itself grew with vengeance. Nima grew alongside it like an ever growing and eternal dunghill. There were sharp land speculators from well-known city families who sold slaves in the past. They moved in, acquired land, and sublet it at murderous rates to the ever growing fugitive population of Nima. But Nima never became permanent. It never will be. There is a long pot-holed street – a forgotten city administrator has had the dirt track sprayed with coal tar in the dim past – which runs through it. The conspicuous landmark is the Harlem Café. Another set is the two septic latrines, a fitting memorial to Nima, the city within a city, Nkrumah once said he would make it. These latrines are ever full. Those in a hurry take a shit right on the floor. Near the septic latrines are huge dunghills which in the language of the Accra City Council are called refuse dumps. No one ever removes refuse in Nima. The long nameless street winds through a collection of tin shacks, mud huts, dodging a fig tree here and there, taking a precarious bend at the entrance of the white mosque with its modest minaret. It continues from the mosque by an open space which serves as a market when the rains are away. Here vultures mingle with the customers and sellers, snatching offal from butchers' stalls and dashing off to the 'refuse dumps' or to the roofs of the public latrines to devour their stolen goods with sad silent faces. This street, if we call it a street, occupies the highest line in Nima. It stretches across a hillock. From its sides run hundreds of lanes made by human feet. These end in deep gulleys in the valley on the edge of the great open gutter. This street comes on in a listless and melancholy manner to the far north of the land. It ends as if by design on the final dunghill which feeds the community's poultry and domestic animals. Women now and then release their beloved little ones to stagger and take a shit on this dunghill. Then the turkeys, chickens, dogs, and ducks descend on the result with venomous rivalry. There is little rotten food thrown away. The by-lanes run in steep slopes, by water pumps where potbellied children, perfect studies in malnutrition, play in the green mud moss growing. Here bare-chested women wheezing with consumption quarrel over who came first in the long winding queue. Now and then the queue will be disrupted by a sturdy driver's mate who needs water to wash his master's car. He will push the women aside, when they protest he will tell them their asses stink, and saunter off with his bucket of water to the cheerful counter-references made to his mother's ass by the women. The houses stand, if they stand, precarious, hurled together by a drunken builder. Mud, zinc, deal board, cardboard, swish. All are bent westward towards the valley and the gutter in the vulgar pose of a woman stripping and bending to take a piss. On the eastern side of Nima, fenced away in respectable seclusion, are the new estate houses of Kanda. Here, the politicians, members of Parliament, directors of public corporations, party functionaries (in those other days, now civil servants have moved in) and a community of well-to-do-prostitutes – who ostensibly work for the national airline or the hotels – live. The hundred by-lanes march with good intention from the street, bend and twist with lunatic suddenness here and there and vanish among the houses whose tops look westward. On the northern part of Nima, beyond the last dunghill, lie violet mountains far away. Serene and smoky after rains, they are distant. On their sides, perched in intellectual arrogance, are the red-top buildings that house the great university. They lie there as if God put them there in His infinite art and wisdom. So that He will then better be able to supervise the building of His new Jerusalem in Nima's green and pleasant fields. They roll away inland beyond the wide valley where prosperous professional people have built trim and smart houses far away from the crowd.

Who are the dwellers of this city within the city? From here, every morning, pour thousands of workers – labourers, carpenters, masons, carriers of night soil, builders, tradesmen, hawkers of petty goods, butchers, pickpockets, soldiers and prostitutes. No one knows exactly how many people live in Nima, in spite of what the Census Office might claim. The 1960 failed to count them for they know that, if you are counted, then you are put down to pay the City Council levy or lampo. During the feverish days of counting, the inhabitants of Nima vanished into the by-lanes, sneaked back to their tumble-down shacks and their grisly beds, twenty to a room, and vanished into the grey dawns of their lives. Every day, as they have done for years, into the city's workshops they poured at dawn to earn a precarious living. The crowd left Nima every day by the mammy trucks, the trotros and open tipper trucks of the foreign companies who sent to collect their workers out of the sharp realization that labour was the basis of all exploitation. Governments never send for their workers. The municipal buses were scarcely seen in Nima for the route is fraught with hazards. The mammy trucks picked up their passengers at dawn near the mosque, and hurtled off in a drunken hurry into the city's work places. There was the eternal line of swarming workers who could never afford the fare, ever winding its way like a primeval python at the world's dark beginning through open green patches by the Ring Road West, vaulting over gulleys and gutters, dodging under barbed wire fences erected by Syrian landowners across their property, and dashing through traffic across a senseless roundabout which used to be for the man they threw out, now for the abstraction for which they threw him out.

From Nima come the washermen, the garden boys and the steward boys of the Ridge bungalows, and of the pretentious suburbia of Kaneshie – those who can afford. From here come the cooks, stewards and drivers of the respectable homes of the city. There are the women of Nima. The hard-working hawking community which sells the early morning koko, beans and gari, kenkey and fish to the workers on tick basis before they dash off on foot or vault into trucks to their daily chores. There are the prostitutes, the night women of Nima; they work in the night clubs that skirt Nima like sorrow children on a dunghill offering respite to its inhabitants, promising them joyous retreats from their earthly worries. Husky-voiced, these women are largely from the rural towns. Illiterate and quarrelsome, they add to the nobility of their profession a capacity to be tough when the occasion demands. Most of them were beautiful once. And young. After years of work, some succeed, amass a tidy wealth, and return home. Others miss the opportunity and the boon – it may be new Lebanese merchants come from Beirut, Italian builders working on the Volta, Japanese sailors from the port town of Tema come upon the city for short squinted dusky diversions. But they linger on, bored, bitter, and disease-ridden, only to wobble to their home towns ill with consumption to die. Others, out of shame, stay on, and die in their soiled bedclothes in airless card and deal board shacks, to be hauled off and buried by their unofficial union or in more desperate circumstances by the City Council Sanitation and Health Department in the pagan section of Awudome Cemetery.

Amamu picked his way carefully that sullen afternoon through faeces human or canine, you cannot tell which, rotten food and puddles of urine, all sending into the hot rising air a chorus of pungent smells and odours. On the first alley behind the mosque, he felt he was near Yaro's house. The air smelled of frying plantain, fish and spices. Along the edges of this leaning alley, four women were frying tatale and plantain, shouting themselves hoarse at urchins in tatters hell bent on theft. He paused to ask one of the urchins who volunteered to lead him there for a fee.

Yaro's house was on the edge of a big gully. Like all the other gullies, it was carved by many rains. Just before the alley swings and bends among the houses, the gully runs on into the depths below with sharp intent. It was a mud house. The gate was made of planks from key-soap packing cases. It was half open. There were in the compound four mud houses menacingly facing each other. An old Moslem was crouching by the side of a short wattle fence washing his testicles with water from a green kettle. The little boy said something to him in Hausa. He turned round slowly, still clutching at his invisible testicles, and pointed to one of the mud houses. As if uninterrupted he proceeded with his ablution with a faraway look.

He knocked on the door on which there were charcoal lines recalling to his mind the sign of the passover. A grunt replied from inside. A little red-eyed boy in the early grips of malaria opened the door. He was naked and clean shaven, dried mango juice on both corners of his mouth.

Where is your papa?

Eh. Ete polis tasen.

Which police station?

Nima.

What is the matter?

Amo n'onklo.

His uncle had been arrested. It was Ibrahim. Yaro had spoken one day about him in a fit of anger. He had come down one day from home. He was a bright-eyed lad of eighteen, if anyone could tell his age. His brother apprenticed him to a tailor who made Hausa gowns near the first refuse dump. Ibrahim did not stay to learn the trade. He hired himself out as a commissionaire to Opera Cinema, a big dark cinema in the heart of the city with a large urchin clientele. Here he made the acquaintance of some of the tough northern boys of Cow Lane, the home of every jockey in the city. Then he started coming home late. Sometimes he would vanish for days and emerge dirty and red-eyed. He had been smoking wee. One day he and Yaro's wife, Ashitu, had a nasty fight in which he clubbed the woman senseless. That was his first brush with the police. But Amamu got him out of the police station and paid the woman's hospital fees. Meanwhile he had lost his job. But he left home every day, came back with stories about his new job at a distillery. Yaro knew it was a lie. He watched out for him. Soon he picked up information that Ibrahim had joined a gang of thieves who were raiding Kanda houses for turkeys, goats, fowls and sheep. The morning after the party, Yaro got home late. His wife told him the police had come and searched the house. They also asked questions about Ibrahim. His box was forced open and searched. They took away a Churchman's cigarette tin full of a brown ground tobacco-like substance. Ibrahim and four of his comrades had been surprised at house number 56 in Kanda the previous night. They had collected fowl and three sheep. They were about to push them under the barbed wire when truncheons fell on them. They were in league with the night watchman. The police were on the beat that night around that area. A police superintendent lived in number 55. The five men were almost literally clubbed to death. They were dragged across the alleys into Nima police station where they were screaming their innocence in four languages.

At five that dawn Yaro rushed to the police station. A constable leaned on the counter in the charge office, dozing. On hearing footsteps he woke up, took a long red look at him and barked, Yes? What you want?

Masa, I beg you, ibe my broder.

Who be your broder?

Masa, dey catch am yestidey. Prosman come for ma house for Nima.

What be im name?

Ibrahim, masa.

The constable moved from the stool, angry. He lurched towards the cells.

Who be Ibrahim? he shouted.

Ibe me, sah.

Come out one tiem.

Ibrahim moved to the cell bars. His blood had caked on his face. His right eye was closed by a lump where his eyebrow once was. The hair on his head was matted by sweat and blood and dirt.

Ibe him? the constable asked no one in particular.

Yes sah, masa, Yaro answered almost in a whisper. He stood there staring at his brother in silent prayer to Allah. Ibrahim stared into the morning outside with his left eye uncertain, unsure.

So whas matter jus now? asked the constable. There was no reply.

Dey catch im yestidey tiefing fowel for Kanda sad. Him and di four piplo who dey insad dere. We git prenty compren; every dey we git compren. We try tey, we no fit catch fo tief. Big big piplo come make compren. We try, we try, we try, we no catch fo tief. Yestidey, Allah dey, we catch evribody. We catch all.

He stopped and gave a short grin. He was enjoying the situation.

Git back dere, tief man lak you, naniama.

Ibrahim painfully moved to the inner part of the cell. Yaro stood there now looking at the floor of the charge office. The constable climbed his stool and resumed his silence.

Masa, I beg you, what I go do?

You be im broder?

Yes sah, masa; same fader no be same moder.

You go git somebody wey sabe book make im come.

Yaro wandered around Nima the whole morning looking for somebody 'who sabe book'. The letter writer under the fig tree refused to go. He was not licensed to be a letter writer. The Ijaw shopkeeper on the second by-lane proclaimed that he sabe book but not very well, as he reached only Standard 'Tree' in his native country. There was Koo the booker at trotro station. No, he didn't want any involvement with the police. No one in Nima ever wants to get involved with the police. Once a lorry loaded with passengers from P.W.D. site ten ran into one of the latrines. The driver had consumed akpeteshie of a quantity enough to be used for a fairly important man's funeral. Some had their legs snapped like twigs, heads were cracked open, ribs were smashed. The scene was blood and screams. But before the police arrived to take 'particulars' all the injured had vanished. The driver had vanished too. They caught him in a shack near the last dunghill incoherently proclaiming his innocence. A few sharp slaps from the corporal restored his sense of vision. He was led to the scene of the accident in a rusty handcuff. There was a large gash on his forehead. No one in Nima wants to get involved with the police. The law is an enemy to these captive people. It means blows administered by its angry representatives. It means fines, handcuffs, tears and blood. It means cells with pans for taking a shit in. It means long waits for trial. It means loss of work, hunger for those left at home.

Yaro by noon was tired in his search for someone who 'sabe book'. He returned to the police station at about one. The constable of the morning had been replaced by a fat-arsed corporal who was studiously writing in a black book, his tongue hanging out.

Whas matter, contri? he barked at Yaro.

I no get no one, masa.

You no get who? You tink ibe play we dey play here?

No sah, masa. Ibe my broder, Ibrahim.

You people are bloody fucking nonsense. Why you Nima people make so much trouble? Tiefman, all, all of you.

With that he returned to his writing, his tongue out following the slow marching of every line.

Yaro went out into the corridor. There he sat down on a bench. There were eight other people sitting there. There was an important-looking man in a Manchester cloth chewing a stick noisily and muttering something in Ashanti to himself. Something about children of today who refuse to listen. There were three men in a row silent as graves. Then a Lagosian woman with child barely a fortnight old whimpering in low moans like a lost cow. On the extreme end sat three other men and a woman whispering in great agitation in Ewe.

Yaro sat down on the nearest edge and waited. He did not know what exactly he was waiting for. Perhaps Allah would show him the way. Allah will. He was turning round an exhausted grind of kola in his mouth. People came and went. Some went into the charge office. Then voices were heard. Then a key would turn and one of the inmates of a cell would emerge, his eyes fiercely red. He would follow the man to a waiting car or taxi and they would speed away on to the Ring Road. Allah will show the way.

Allah did show his way. Amamu arrived at the station. Yaro got up from the bench and dashed forward to his master.

Masa, Allah dey, masa, Allah dey, he kept on saying. Then he told a long confused story. Amamu walked up to the charge office counter. The corporal was still writing in his black book. He lifted his head up when he felt someone had come in.

Yes sir, what can I do for you? he asked.

You have a young man here called Ibrahim?

Yes, I think so, sir.

I want to bail him.

So? The corporal became angry. He was polite to this man because he wore a tie. But that didn't entitle him to speak with such arrogance.

And who be you?

I am lawyer. . . .

Oh, that's right, sah. Sorry, sah. O.K., sah. Right away, sah.

A lawyer is next to God. He is the one who gets you out of trouble; he is the one who puts you into trouble. If you steal a thing and you are caught, get a lawyer; he is clever. He will argue with 'them' and you will go free. He is the one who can talk with the law. And the police respect him. He is the one who can say anything to the police. And they can't touch him. Because he knows the law. He knows all, he himself will tell you what lies to tell. That is why when they die they put their faces downwards.

He stood near the counter as the corporal went to call his boss, a sad-eyed inspector who appeared to be agitated but managed to keep the composure that was characteristic of law enforcement people everywhere.

He arrived at the station just a few minutes before word came from Korle Bu Hospital. Ibrahim had started vomiting blood at about eleven o'clock. A black Maria had rushed him, with a police escort, to the hospital after his brother's first visit. He died an hour later of internal haemorrhage, due to severe injuries caused by a heavy blunt instrument which had damaged his kidneys. The body was in the mortuary. Would the lawyer and the nearest relative care to go to the hospital to identify the body? The inspector was polite and gentle.

Yaro followed his master the rest of that afternoon like a sleepwalker, muttering something in his native tongue. At the mortuary, the attendant opened the big fridge. There was a doctor nervously rubbing his palms together and mumbling. It was too late when they brought him, it was too late.

Amamu arrived home late that evening. The house was deserted. Alice had left for Cape Coast.

He slumped in a chair. Then he realized that Yaro was still standing there in the living room.

What is the matter, Yaro?

Nothing, sah, my brother ibe him e die.

Go and bury him.

Yes sah, masa, I go go bury am. Yes sah.

He picked his way gingerly, as if reluctant to hurt the earth with his footfall.

# ••• *Chapter 12a*

> The Negroes, upon seeing the destruction and utter ruin of their sacred Rocks, meanwhile believed that they were looking upon the loss of all hope of their salvation, and all eagerly and in a great rage took up their arms and so struck hard at the workmen, who not being able to resist them retreated in flight to the boats.
>
> Ruy de Pina. *The Building of Elmina Castle* (1482)

In war, if anyone kills an enemy, he beheads him and puts his head in a bag to bring home. Thereby it will be known how many foes he slew. But if they shoot someone, and he falls down with his face to the heavens, it is a taboo to cut off his head, for it is believed that whoever cuts off his head will be plagued to death by the ghost of the dead foe. The heads are well dried, and brave people drink from them on great occasions. Some of them adorn famous drums.

And tomorrow, the fields shall be hoed by naked-to-the-waist stalwarts from the grassland for a fee that can scarcely keep them alive. The trucks shall hurtle them through the grassland into the construction sites to lay stone upon stone for the owners.

The maxim is: the labourer is worthy of his hire and nothing more.

Here is visible a ring of low blue hills smoking after the tropical rain.

The reconciliation of the Bull and the Man cannot be achieved now, for there are a million ancestral crimes that must be atoned for.

In the hills the bullfrogs are wailing a song a death chant without unison without focus.

For tears will fill the land again, and the survivors will be accountable to God, the Christian God, alone.

We hear the new mourning cries, and we ask, Was there no mourning earlier, is it a new death, a renewal of the funeral obsequies?

The Lebanese merchants are bargaining away native lands; even a government that proclaims socialism – a confusion of ideas beliefs and magic – cannot provide the answer. So the children turn beggars in the market place, as the eminent men play golf on the Achimota course. The best golf course in the country.

In the Senior Common Room, the scholars of the land are debating international communism, and providing new arguments for Fabianism that died in its country of origin. It is a mark that they went to Oxford, so European socialists who seek any interest in the ideological matters of Africa are discredited prophets in their own country. They should practise socialism in their own countries.

The beer is good; there are two excellent breweries and one is soon to be built in the Western Provinces to brew wholesome beer for the people.

Meanwhile drinking water is short in the north and in the Ewe country.

The International Dining Club is holding a banquet in the city. Eminent people will address the diners on the significant importance of international finance. Evening dress is compulsory.

'I shall make Nima a City within a City.' Meanwhile ministers are acquiring twenty-three houses, and buying gold beds, and the Leader will make a Dawn Broadcast. One man one car is a negative slogan!

And she whom I followed to come here has gone away into the ocean. She the orphan is lost among the storm.

It is not possible to deny the potency of logic – Hope says it is equivalent to magic – in the conceptualization of one single simple predicament. Anger is futile, for death maybe is the only reality.

And perchance to dream, there is the rub.

In the traditions of the clan, dreams have a signification that cannot be grasped by the Western mind. The concept of angels is a total fiction for they and devils – evil ones – are one and the same.

When the Brigadier quotes the Nunc Dimittis he is lamenting the futility of it all.

The civil service is the most selfless institution that ensures the continuity of the nation. It has a long untarnished record of devoted service. It has among its ranks some of the most illustrious sons of the land.

At a Moslem burial, no coffins are used. This must be considered very dangerous to public health, as rats may carry plague from the putrefaction, and thereby pollute the drinking water of the city. The Moslems must be made to use coffins in their burial ceremonies. The City Council must see to the enforcement of this by-law. We shall call it By-law 98/2 Section 10. Long Live Parliamentary Democracy.

One of the new leaders said if elected he would build a welfare state in which there will be unemployment benefit for workers, a graduated tax system, children allowance, free medical service, and above all drinking water for the rural areas.

The land falls at the edge of the forest in a sharp decline, and here gravel pits abound. When the construction workers dug there for gravel, they came upon burial chambers of ancient kings and rulers reposing in a long cool corridor of earth held up by stalwart odum props. The National Archives must intervene in order to save this historical site which may in the future serve as a tourist attraction.

We have many beautiful places in the country to which tourists especially Americans, who will pay to see anything, can be lured with the appropriate posters and publicity material.

Behind those gullies, the people squat and defecate with an extraordinarily easy conscience.

The churches and the cathedrals are the most solid-looking buildings in the area – you get the same impression in Bali – they are made of stones while the dwelling houses of the people are a collection of crude mud houses designed to last exactly one tropical rain, and then must collapse under the erosive power of the torrential downpour. But the poor devils don't seem to mind. How they live in those things cannot be imagined.

Our sadness itself, based upon that distant sadness which is the history of this land, defies all consolation. Those nearer to the edge of the hills can see far out to the ocean where the Greek salt merchant has his salt pans, and can, like the Brigadier, sing Nunc Dimittis.

When I told them that young Africans left secondary schools speaking Latin and Greek they thought it was one of those fantastic African lies. All Africans are congenital liars. Othello was a liar.

All of us are sleepwalkers, some walk a little faster than others. We will scream in the papers if they sell the Pharmaceutical Corporation to a company from Illinois. Meanwhile the nation is dying on its knees, dying in its own defecation.

Then they will talk of brotherly love, of international understanding to the sharp financiers clutching their briefcases.

And Freddie Thompson shouted on the tarmac: I am being sold into slavery a second time! By the gods of Africa I am being sold again. I came back after three hundred years. And ye gods of Africa, I am being sold into slavery a second time!

Poor Freddie. They rescued him, so that he could become a floor manager in an Italian furniture factory. He is a very good carpenter.

Christ was a carpenter too. But they nailed him to his own cross with nails and hammers from his own toolbox.

I saw her leave the moonlight doorway shut with the wave. I saw her clutch her gods in a foreign manner. She vanished where the moon cuts the sea into two.

Will she not come again?

Lovers in the dunghill gardens holding hands in the manner of the Aladuras flowing through the midnight streets.

We will be caught in the simple logic of survival again and again. What a futile struggle.

On the hill the emancipated academics will debate the question of academic freedom – freedom to think academically, to pursue intellectual work without let or hindrance. The university must be autonomous in the fullest sense of the word.

I too want to believe.

Then the memory of her my lover torments me like the gnats and flies when the mango tree is flowering by Christmas at home, as my dog lay dying in the gutter where a fire truck had laid it to rest. The elements will take on the colour of her beads – the red of the prize cock and the green of the avia, and the blue of the dyer's palm. Venom in blood must flow in this land before a burial ground will be prepared by the last and final dunghill.

Man endures the inevitable yoke in the mistaken belief

preached by the Christian's Holy Book that there is a resting place beyond these hills beyond these fields.

That summer of my flight to Europe in search of her I saw once in Stockholm the whisky-drinking girl studying African anthropology demanding answers to questions on tribal customs and burial ceremonies.

Munyi says that he believed that cannibalism was still being practised among the European tribes.

The night itself stretched like a blood-red pennant, proclaiming that the pentagon of the rulers shall recede, recede like the lagoon once upon a harmattan season when fishes were marooned upon the salt earth. These shall be collected to feed the starving children.

At the feast of the Ramadan, Ahmadu el Said shall scream quotations from the Holy Koran on the grassy plains facing the Ambassador Hotel where the infidels are preparing a great feast of untouchable meat. El Said, fat and oily in his brief Moslem ablutions, believes in one simple truth – the holiness of Allah, even in the hour of his death.

Under the trees, the devout followers of Allah are praying, their faces, denuded of all joy in hunger and emaciation, turned benevolently towards Mecca. The prayer is a low monotone – for the fast has drained the vocal cords of all saliva – gurgling in a throaty snarl against Allah the Benevolent One.

My woman of the sea, I am leaving for the almond tree where I first met you. I shall be there when you rise, when you rise to meet me at our appointed hour. I am coming down from these mountains of dung from these hills of shame. I shall walk the steps of ancient war drums, I shall move to the beat of husago, atrikpui and agbadza in the twirl of my folded cloth you will read the sign of my coming. My lips will be sealed so I cannot sing those ancient songs. I will believe you when you say you will come into the same fields I rode with the ghosts the first memorials of my journey from the womb. For now believe me, the land is covered with blood, and more blood shall flow in it to redeem the covenant we made in that butterfly field, and under my almond. For you I renounce the salvation of madness and embrace with a singular hope, your hope. You will dance again in my time our time the same step you traced in the earth to the ancient drums, and through them reveal the eternal legend of your love. I shall crawl to your knees in the sand at the water's edge and retrace then the first syllables of my speech.

I am looking for her where will I find who among you can tell me where to find her who among you can point the place where she went.

They are searching under the shrubs for the spirits of the departed priests of thunder. The drums themselves are muffled now by the anguish of the drummers lost in trance among the nims.

Nye dzi akpo dzidzo le xexeame fe numadinuwo nuti eye nye aseyetsotso ade gbefa nye sitsofe dede. Miadometo kawoe awo kale le anyigba sia dzi, aha tutu adatsi le mo na ahosiwo maha?

It shall be the last and singular act that you will perform for her memory, the finite prostration shall signify one simple act of faith – that her return shall be proclaimed before the second cock in the land.

We will keep the faith that heavenly muskets shall sound her coming.

So the cry must go up for her my loved one she with the black nipples and a tooth extracted long long dead in her twelfth year of witches eating her intestines. Her disappearance beneath the waves was her final farewell. The shrines are falling now, the fences have been eaten by termites.

Return the miracle return the miracle return the miracle.

## ••• *Chapter 13*

His headache had come again this evening. Throbbing, violent, as if many drums and gongs and rattlers were playing there. There was a jerkiness, a pumping regularity in all things as he watched them. The walls seemed to shiver in different lights. The chains assumed different forms now and then jumping up. There was a brightness in the light of day outside. He must sit down.

He sat. Slowly and calmly he moved towards the chest of drawers on the right. There was half a bottle of scotch. He poured himself a long drink. His hand shook as he lifted it to his lips. It was bitter and harsh on his palate. He gulped it down and literally threw the glass on the side table.

Things began to jump again. First a faint breeze caught the white curtain on the large back window. It lifted it gently, then raised it in a wide arc fluttering it like a furled flag on a distant flagpole. Slowly, it caressed it, brought it down to the sill. A faint ripple persisted, as the curtain sadly rested, tried to rest, on the sill. Then a bright light caught the dining table right in the centre. It had a blue spot to it. It rested for a while in a violent glimmer. He had never seen a light like this before. The drums and the gongs and the rattlers had resumed their play in his head with a regular syncopation. They were playing a weird drum beat of his childhood, a medicine drum. The light rose from the centre of the table and began to dance a quick dance. Suddenly it stopped. The drums went into a slow funereal beat of mourning. Faintly a voice emerged singing a dirge. It was the voice of someone he knew. But he could not remember. Someone close to him. His mother? His grandmother? It was a distinct female voice singing a dirge about the day of death, of trees withered, of leaves fallen from the evergreen baobab, of a desert storm, of skulls crossing a wide impenetrable expanse of forest soaked in the desert rain. Then a voice began to talk about the searcher who finds, the searcher who finds in the wilderness the death that will kill him, the sorrow of the pallbearers, the pity he will have for them who will carry his body to the grave. The song stopped. The drums and the gongs and the rattlers resumed the medicine beat. And from nowhere the light emerged again, this time dancing on the wall opposite him.

It was a classroom now. They were reading the Primer One. Ata has my cap, repeat after me, Ata has my cap. S, O, so, G, O, go, is he to go in? on on we go; repeat after me, S, O, so. Medicine men were gathered at an airport. An aeroplane was to take off. They were talking excitedly of a swindler who had sold a plot of land to three people. They were holding talismans and mouthing incantations. Fall for me to take, fall, coconut fall for me to take. Dogs, dogs. Ata has my cap, S, O, so, G, O, go; is he to go in? On on we go.

He rose up from the chair. He unlaced his shoes, loosened his tie and stepped out into the evening.

## ••• *Chapter 14*

The search for him began on the third day. People who had appointments with him stood outside his door for hours. Clients turned up in court expecting to see his familiar figure striding among the flower pots in pensive quietude. He was gone. Friends at the club were wondering where he'd gone to. People went to Adisa. No, she hadn't seen him. She had telephoned his office and no reply.

When he stepped out into the evening three days ago, his steps led him to the Circle. He had no shoes on. He was in a pair of striped trousers and a sleeveless singlet. Around the Circle, the City Council had planted a park some time ago. Here, whenever the army band felt good, it sometimes came and played selections from Glenn Miller to a crowd of half-starved labourers. It was part of the government's plan to bring music to the people. Work and Happiness.

The band had swung into 'At the Woodchopper's Ball' when he arrived. He mingled with the crowd. He pushed through to the second circle, swaying to the music of massed instruments – the trombones wailing and trumpets whistling in a shrill syncopation with horns and drums. He swayed his head for a while, and started to conduct the way he knew it should be done. Those who stood near him moved away. He was in the first circle now swinging his arms in a fury of baton acrobatics the way he'd seen a great conductor do in the Royal Albert Hall.

After conducting for about two minutes, he became bored. When he started to move away, the band had struck up another tune, this time a quick martial song popular during the war. He tore his way into the crowd as if pursued.

He paused at the edge of the crowd. There were still a few empty benches under the pride of Barbados plants. He made for one. He sat down and broke into sweat. It wasn't very hot, but he was sweating profusely.

The music floated in the air, now caught in the screech of tyres negotiating the Circle. He still had his socks on. After a while, a group of children came and sat by him. There were six of them. One took a multicoloured handkerchief out of a dirty pocket. He was looking at him. He collected three pieces of pebbles and tied them on to the handkerchief. There is a cement path that runs through the green grass. He threw the knotted handkerchief on the path. Then they all retired and sat near him. He was smiling now. First an old man walked by. His feet kicked the knotted handkerchief. But he went his way. The children ran and picked up the handkerchief. Now they placed it more centrally in the path. A woman with a baby on her back waddled along. Her feet knocked it. She paused, looked at the knotted handkerchief. She turned round and went her way. Then a young sturdy worker came along. He was enjoying the game with the children. He was smiling to himself and at the handkerchief. The young worker's eyes caught the knotted handkerchief. He paused in his long stride. He bent down slowly and picked it up. He raised himself up, and looked left and right to see if anyone saw him. Then he pocketed his find hurriedly and proceeded in his long strides. The children burst out in a scream and chased after him.

It is ours, please, it is ours, they cried.

What is yours?

The handkerchief.

The worker pulled the handkerchief from his pocket.

This one?

Yes, chimed the children now laughing uncontrollably.

What is in it? asked the young man.

Money, our father sent us with it, the children said. The young worker untied the handkerchief. He saw the pebbles. In a flash he got hold of one of the children, their leader, and began to cuff him on the ear. The rest had run away laughing. After a while he released him, and proceeded on his way with the children screaming insults at him.

He was amused very much. He laughed and laughed, for a long time. He caught himself suddenly. He must be on his way. He crossed the Nsawam Road at where a woman sold rice and stew with cement paper. He walked very swiftly past the Lido, and kept to the edge of the road for the roads of this city have no sidewalk. When he was opposite the Nima police station where he had been at noon, he broke into a trot. He kept the trot on till he reached Survey School where he paused. On the park near the Survey School, a rally of some sort was going on. He saw someone screaming something about the right of workers to strike for just wages, and the right of workers to hold their jobs economic crisis or no economic crisis. Full employment must be guaranteed. He strolled around the rally for about ten minutes. Soon he set out on his way.

Night was now falling fast. Cars were speeding fast towards the airport. Car lights caught him now and then full in the face. He paused near Legion Village, home of disabled soldiers who fought in Burma, and pissed into their cassava farm. At the junction where the road goes to the airport, he turned right. Soon sweat-covered, he entered the airport hotel. Those who were sitting on the veranda were looking at him.

Can I buy one bottle club beer? he said.

The man gave him a bottle opened. He counted many pieces of coins from his pocket, and started walking away.

You must consume it on the premises, the man said as if addressing someone behind him. He put the beer to his mouth, and took a long pull. It choked him as he removed it from his mouth. A long spurt of foam shot on to the counter. He turned round and walked into the road. He crossed at the zebra crossing, very carefully, he walked off to the railings enclosing the tarmac. Aeroplanes were taking off zoom zoom, any time they zoomed off he also shouted, Zoom! After a while aeroplanes were taking off again.

He turned round suddenly and walked away. Night was falling fast, and he must be on his way.

He hit the main Accra–Denu road finally at about ten o'clock. He was full of energy. He was strong. He didn't feel the sharp gravel of the road cut into the soles of his feet through the socks. Sweat was pouring down his face. He kept as much as he could to the side of the road, sometimes he moved to the grassland, and walked swiftly with long strides. Cars passed him, a mammy truck nearly knocked him down at one point. He did not hear when the driver cursed him.

He walked the whole night. He didn't pause anywhere. Only once when he stopped and pissed into another cassava farm near Ada junction. Now and then as he passed silent villages, dogs raised a din upon hearing his footsteps. At Dawa two hunting dogs rushed from the nearest house into the village. When they came near him about three yards they stopped, and just growled in a soft hum. He didn't even notice them. At one time, around midnight, he saw a single light far away in the plain. After the light had flickered for a while, it went out. Then he heard three gun shots. That was a hunter.

At about five he arrived at Tefle. Trucks were lined up this side of the river. The passengers, the drivers and their mates were sleeping. The place was quiet. He slipped under the barrier and headed towards the water. When his feet hit the water, a sudden thirst thrust through his throat, and he fell upon his knees.

After a long drink of water, he washed his face, and pissed into the water. It occurred to him that he could not cross the river. So he must wait and take the ferry. It left at six.

In the city, panic was spreading. Sammy had started the search for him around six. A nagging awareness and unease kept tugging at his heartstrings. He was alive, he thought safe somewhere. Maybe at Adisa's. He had been to his house in the early afternoon. He just wanted to stop by for a drink. The house was deserted. The main door was open. He looked around in the living room. The feeling came over him that he was somewhere just around the corner, just walked over to a neighbour's. Or someone had stopped by and they had gone for a drink. He closed the door and left.

Later in the evening he drove by. There was no one at home. He drove to the club. Almost all the regulars were there. Old Row sat in the right-hand corner, a beer mug in his hand, belching contentedly after his tenth drink. Bob was regaling a group with some readily concocted story about a woman caught in adultery in his home town in 1936; one or two very important-looking top civil servants, one had a face like a half-effaced penny piece and a piping voice. He walked up to Richard perched on his long stool behind the counter, humming a forgotten tune from his native rivers.

You see lawyer, Richard?

No sir, masa; e no come today.

He wanted to stop awhile and have a drink; but this was not his crowd. Besides he was very junior in the service; he must not push himself into the midst of these demigods of the administration. He must go to Adisa's house.

She was home. She wore a simple frock with several yellow butterflies playing in a sunny field, there were a few children too, chasing the butterflies. She was sitting in the large locally made armchair. The door was half open. She was holding a jar of pomade which she was rubbing gently and absent-mindedly into her hair.

Hey, Sammy, welcome and shall I ask what?

She paused. With her woman's intuition she knew that something was wrong. She could tell from his eyes. There was a subdued light that shone with tiny flickers of perceivable hope. Their usual fresh and joyous brightness had been overcast by a little but deep cloud. They communicated a certain alarm.

Is something wrong? What has happened?

I went by: he was not there.

Well, that is not too bad.

But his main door was open. And Yaro was nowhere. I went back after hours. And still no one. I closed the door.

What about his wife?

Her room was empty. The curtains from the windows have been removed. And there were no sheets on the beds.

Did you go to the regular bars?

Yes, and I . . .

What is it? Please tell me. What is it?

Then they both fell silent for what looked like many days, with nights of doubt and dreams intervening between bright light-headed hours of pouring sunshine without shadows or shades. Then she spoke. First quietly in a low monotone, a voice Sammy had never heard before. It was a voice that beat low and moved only on one tonal plane, explosively subdued in its sorrow. It was like the low crying of a mother hen whose chicks a hawk has snatched. It was the plaintive cry of a lonely mother bitch whose puppies a truck smashed on the asphalt road in midtown.

I don't know what it is, but I feel it, here on my heart. It is a pain. A pain. Something . . .

She went on in this vein, in this voice. There were no tears in that voice. None. It was level. When she finished speaking she waved her right hand in front of her eyes, as if she were clearing a malingering cobweb. It was a quick brief wave.

She moved towards the plastic wardrobe; she removed a dress from it. She began to dress very carefully; very slowly and deliberately she dressed. Sammy sat watching her every movement. When she finished, she turned round.

Let us go.

They did not tell each other where they were going. The night was dark, night darkens in the city early; it was lit by twinkling oil lamps from the pork sellers' stalls.

Sammy decided to drive to the university, to the Senior Common Room where he used to hang out with school friends who had become respected academics spouting brilliant clichés from books. They approached this centre of learning very gingerly. Voices hit them from the courtyard where around a wide moonlit centre table the learned ones of the land were drinking and discussing knotty academic points.

Sammy approached one bald one with dirty nostrils. He had met him on one drunken windy Saturday afternoon with Amamu.

No, I haven't seen him. Have you tried the Tiptoe? Everyone knows that is his second home.

This was greeted with hearty guffaws.

He drove blindingly through the ill-lit streets of the city. He drove to the homes of some of his friends. He drove to night clubs, to bars tucked away among trees in forgotten sections of town where there were no roads. He drove through banana groves to night clubs he had not known ever existed. He drove to the big hotels where Europeans were drinking on terraces and all the Africans you saw there were only servants; he drove to out-of-town motels designed exclusively for extramarital romance. He drove to Nima in search for Yaro.

But he didn't know the house. Adisa remembered where it was, but rather vaguely because she did not get out of the car one afternoon when Amamu dropped Yaro because it was raining.

A little boy near the mosque showed them the house. A little boy with dried mango juice on the corners of his mouth and on his belly large with terminal malnutrition. A small group was gathered in Yaro's compound. They had just come back from the cemetery. They were silent. Everyone stared at the visitors but quickly returned to his or her mourning. A woman's voice came from the room in the back singing a northern dirge.

They gave them chairs. Suddenly without warning Adisa began to cry. No one knew why. They thought perhaps she knew Ibrahim, and his death had overwhelmed her. One woman was wailing in a monotone, dramatic with sorrow. And I sold him some koko and akara only yesterday morning. Yie, yie, he came to me and said, Mammy, I want to buy some koko and akara. I with my own hands, I dished out the koko into a calabash for him; it was one of the new calabashes my sister sent from Gambaga. I wrapped for him four pieces of akara in an old newspaper. He paid me in coppers, six coppers he put into this withered palm of mine and made for the shade of the fig tree near the mosque. And today he is not here. We planted him; he is the seed we planted; the seed that will not germinate. We come from so far away to this place, O my fathers, we come from so far away. With that she burst into an uncontrollable sob.

Adisa was still crying, a cry now without voice. Tears flowed on her cheeks, washing the rouge she had so painstakingly applied in one little onward-marching rivulet down her cheeks on to her chin, and dripped upon her kaba.

Yaro emerged from the shadows somewhere. He crouched beside Sammy, a vacant look on his face. There was no worry there now. No apprehension, no pain. All was drained away. A nervous calmness had settled upon him. He suddenly looked old; he wore for the first time an indeterminable age, an oldness that was not time's, an agedness of hills and rivers. In that what was the true and more valid self of this peasant turned into a squatter on the dunghill of modern Africa was a final weariness that defied all description. They talked in whispers.

You see your master today, Yaro?

Yes, I see am.

What time you see him?

About tree o'crock tiem. Me an him go for aspiti go tiek my broder in body for motri. Yes, ibe tree o'crock tiem; if I no lie, e lef small mek the tiem catch tree o'crock. Wes matter, masa?

Nothing. We are just looking for him.

Something wrong, masa? Masa? A slow animation had come back to his face. He was suddenly the eternal servant, solicitous about his master. For him the responsibility towards Amamu was almost religious; it was something for which in the distant hereafter he would be called upon by Allah to give account. He knew with that desperate instinct that transcends blood that something terrible had happened. It had to do with a doom, a catastrophe, a total collapse of all things, his world, his all, a catastrophe of which the seed they planted that afternoon in the Moslem section of Awudome Cemetery was only the beginning.

Sammy led Adisa towards the rickety gate held together by wires from packing cases, its deal and cardboard battered by many a determined marauding army of goats and sheep.

The night was thick. Adisa cried silently as they drove. For her, this was the end. The journey out of degradation had ended. His majestic simplicity had been the basis of his love for her. Somewhere she knew that the source of that love was no more. She would never see him again. Somewhere in the distance, across her memories of childhood and her native land, she heard a voice calling her home, to come home, hurry home now that evening had come. Their love was almost divine; its power was quiet and wordless. His loneliness and restlessness became part of her sacred responsibilities, for which she devised ritual acts of celebration and worship and sacrifice. This love was beyond the corporate confusion that hammered at his gates daily. They swore no oaths. Their love was silent. Life itself was too mean a price to pay for this communion. She burst into tears, sobbing tears.

They drove into the night of their mutual loss and solitude. The world had come to a silent end in this dark tropical light.

The dawn had cleared into a bright morning over the shiny

Volta. Passengers, drivers and their mates had woken up. There was a din and confusion as people rushed to the river to wash their faces, and prepare for the journey onwards. Some were going so far as Lagos. Some were going to Cotonou, some Lome, some Niamey, others were going to Keta and its surrounding villages.

He sat by the bank of the river. His sweat had dried up in the morning wind. His mouth was dry. Then he heard truck engines being revved up. The gate was open now. The launch which had slept at the other bank started slowly towards this side. After an eternity it arrived. He was the first to get on the launch. A man in black coat, the remainder of his uniform of office, gave him a ticket. He didn't have any money left after he paid for his beer at the airport hotel. Where are you going? Silence. Can't you hear? He stood staring at him. Go on, on with your troubles, as for you these people, it's too early to mind you at all, even one penny you want to tief it.

Tu tu tu tu tu tu the launch churned through the water slowly, held on to its path by overhead cables. The tide was low. The landing was difficult. After a series of trials amidst yells and shouts by the engine men and the crew, it finally hit the wooden planks on the other side. He lurched forwards and jumped on to the plank.

A new fire seemed to have entered him as he dashed off in a trot under the road block and headed into the straight road that tapers among lost coconuts and distant villages.

At Dabala junction, he broke his trot into a steady stride. He threw his head back and breathed the air smelling of burned grass and lagoon water. Soon lorries started passing him. Some hooted their horns to see if he would stop and get in for a shilling. But he was not aware of them. He strode easily. His feet were sore now, his pair of socks having been torn and eaten away by the rough road. But he was not aware of pain. He was not tired. His walk was more brisk than when he started.

He began to meet farmers on their way to farm, women with wares on their heads heading for the market at Monenu. They all took a quick look at him and stepped aside for him to pass on his way. He didn't see them.

About eleven he arrived at Denu. He made straight for the

beach. He continued his journey along the seacoast. Where fishermen's nets stretched to sea he bent and passed underneath them. The edges of his trousers were now wet, and loaded with sand at where they were folded. Fishermen shouted greetings to him which he didn't hear. Once or twice he paused to look at catches of fish – mackerel nets as fish jumped into the smell of fishermen's sweat. But he went on. The sand impeded his progress because it was a long time since he had walked in the sand, since he had walked upon the beach with bare feet. He had taken off his wet pair of socks and his blistered feet sank into the yellow sand, and his footprints receded with the backwards and forwards surge of the Atlantic surf.

He arrived when the church bell on the mission compound was chiming twelve.

He made for the almond tree. It was gnarled and old with age now. It was however in leaf. Its roots – buttressed into the sand – had been picked clean by the advancing sea. But it still rested above the little sand cave where he used to wash for gold dust.

He sat down at its feet gazing out to sea. A sudden calmness descended upon him.

He was a boy of eight. His father had decided he must go and live with some people from the interior now in a town on the coast. His sister was barely four, a lean wispy girl with a sad face whom he loved and beat very often. The day had come and he must go away from the bosom of his mother whom he loved. His mother did not agree. Her husband's word was law. A carpenter friend of his father's had made him a chop-box, a rough job made of sardine packing cases. Into this he arranged his few clothes neatly, between sniffs and bursts of crying. He wore a yellow shirt made of imitation silk. He had bought the cloth with money saved from selling snails to Lagos women, and shelled palm nuts to the U.A.C. produce buyer with the wheezing chest and a squint. This he wore over a pair of white drill shorts his mother had made for him last Easter when they came back from his grandfather's funeral. He wore no shoes. He was not to wear them till he was sixteen. Suddenly he began to cry. He was clutching a loaf of sixpenny sugar bread. The children of the household led him to the lorry that was to carry him away. His mother and everyone began to cry. She sobbed convulsively. His father became annoyed at the wailing. He hoisted him into the lorry with a curse. The lorry sped away into the dust and the future.

He had arrived home at last. The Atlantic breakers boomed across the memory of years; sea gulls careered upwards and downwards above the surf, and rose and crashed into the sand like the madman at the rise of a new moon. The tumult was the signal for the calm that was promised, it was the legend of a final peace.

Then slowly he saw her, the woman of the sea, his cousin love of those years long long ago rising from the sea. She rose slowly, head first, adorned with sapphires, corals and all the ancient beads her mother left for her pubertal rites. She rose slowly from a dream sea. The sea was real: the sun was beating down hard and cruel. It was like a scene in that waking dream of fever. It seemed suddenly that the centuries and the years of pain of which he was the inheritor, and the woes for which he was singled out to be carrier and the sacrifice, were being rolled away, were being faded in that emergence. Here at last, he realized with a certain boyish joy, was the hour of his salvation. It was coming at last. She rose now up upon the waves, her breasts bare, her nipples blacker than ever. On her face a little smile; the sun gave out a radiance that recalled the bright sunshine of the butterfly fields and the hunt of childhood and her first epiphany. There an eerie silence clung to the earth and the sea, over the memorial booms of the ceaseless waves echoes of the muskets of her funeral procession. In the company of one lonely gorgeous star she rose. She walked on the sand, her arms outstretched; she strode towards him, a smile on her face; her breasts bobbing softly. From his island of solitude and joy, utter indescribable joy, he moved towards her. She was there standing in front of him. He sank upon his knees. She enveloped him in her warm embrace. Her smell was of cinnamon and wild flowers, ancient smells of treasure well kept for the children of the future.

They found him kneeling in the sand, a vacant look and a smile and a joy upon his face. And the waves beat their eternal notes upon the shore, as they washed against his body.

The old man arrived in the city at noon the following day. Yes, he received the telegram. He was met by Sammy and Adisa at the lorry park.

He is missing? How can a grown man be missing? First they must make a complaint at the police station. Yes, they knew him. Wasn't he the tall lawyer who lived in Kaneshie? He would turn up. They should all go home. He would be angry if he heard a complaint had been lodged about him missing. He would be very very angry. Wasn't it the lawyer they were talking about? He would turn up. Everybody must go home and sleep.

Children playing on the beach saw him under the Indian almond. People from his household came. It was the third day. The old man had returned from the city. He also came and saw him. He was not asleep now. He was gazing out to sea, a sad quixotic smile on the face. His eyes were blazing. He didn't seem to notice anyone. He was not aware of anyone.

## ••• *Chapter 15*

The taxi pulled up near the gates of the Young Men's Christian Association. The old man sat silent, chewing his gums. He did this whenever he was in pain. Not physical pain. Whenever there was a death that touched him too deeply for words he chewed his gums. The old woman, battered by years of hard work and suffering, stared silently at the buildings. She never said a word. Her mouth now hung loose, controlled in a silent tautness that was beyond endurance.

Rain had fallen a few hours earlier. The ground was wet, drenched in with the fallen leaves of the nim. There was that sickly smell of the nim when the cure for fever was boiling, rising with its vapour from the earth. A little way off there rose another smell, this time of burning fish. A woman was chanting, Come and buy fish, come and buy fish. A group was practising hymns in the courtyard of the Y.M.C.A. They might have moved indoors when the rain came. They had now come out into the bright afternoon sun of the courtyard to tell the world.

Who would true valiant be
Let him come hither.

The hymn floated silently, tossed now and then by the echoes. It now came from the large pit where they say a crocodile lives. Now it came from the valley beyond the building over the deep valley across the forest of nims into Nima:

There's no discouragement
Will make him once relent
His first avowed intent
To be a pilgrim.

It was an all-male group. Christian youth singing with a fervour that engulfed them into the bright setting sun

The taxi turned around. The old man and the old woman walked towards the place. At the end of the road on which they were was a little sad roundabout designed and built by an engineer who had forgotten what it was he was commemorating. Farther on the right stood the Holy Trinity Cathedral with its stained-glass windows telling stories of Christ's journey to Calvary, telling of another sorrow. Faintly, an organ came through the nim trees playing a hymn. A priest walked, walked to and fro in front of the cathedral, his cross bigger than Christ's on the way to Calvary.

They stopped by the gate. A man in khaki suit came. After a brief exchange they were led in. They did not raise their voices above a whisper. They stepped into the courtyard. There was a big building that sprawled on all sides, facing an empty courtyard swept clean by the previous rain. On the sides below the wall were flowers, tropical flowers struggling in a mess, struggling to make the wall. On the right-hand side of the yard was an area as large as a tennis court, closed in by tall iron railings. This was the women's section. There were women on the tennis court. Some were naked reclining on the cement floor with their eyes towards heaven. Some stood in their nakedness looking at passers-by with unuttered prayers in their eyes. Some were running, chasing one another in a childlike game of blind man's buff. Some just sat and chattered in many tongues. There was one who sat near the gate of the enclosure, naked but for a small piece of cloth covering her lower abdomen. She was young, must be about eighteen, and beautiful. Her hands were between her legs, covering her womanhood. Through her fingers her pubic hair poured in riotous abandon. Her gaze was fixed on the old man and the old woman. Then she gave a scream, a long shrill scream from some forgotten nightmare. Her voice rose in a hysterical pitch. Two attendants came and led her away.

The old couple walked on leaving their footfalls behind. They turned into another gate. From here they entered a corridor on the side of which were iron railings. In it were the men. Some were in chains, moaning, some just sat, some were singing undefinable songs you felt you had heard before.

They were led by an attendant into a small room, cheaply furnished with two armchairs and a centre table on which stood n empty glass vase. The old people stood. After some time, the ttendant returned with a small man with rimless spectacles from hich his eyes glinted with misty kindness.

The old man sat down clutching his panama hat in both hands. hen he spoke. His voice sounded like those ghosts moaning at ight from the seashore whenever there was storm and rain and inds, when as children you were afraid lying shivering in your eds, and you remembered the cold wetness of the cemetery from here ghosts came to fish at sea on stormy nights.

The doctor, the small man was a doctor, went out for a while. Ie brought back a pile of papers, a set of clothes and a black otebook.

These are his things. I am really sorry about everything. Ord- rly, tell them that I knew him personally, he was a brilliant wyer, but some of these things do happen. Most of the time we annot understand.

The orderly repeated the doctor's words in the language of the ld man and the old woman. They listened silently. Then the old ıan shook hands with the doctor and said thank you, and added mething about only God knowing. The doctor, having seen eath too many times to be upset, showed a surprising mood of rrow to this old couple. The old woman didn't shake hands. The rderly packed the clothes into a neat bundle and wrapped news- apers around it. The little notebook he gave to the old man, the arcel to the old lady.

They rose up and walked through the gates of the grey build- ıg. The organ from the cathedral was still playing the same missal ymn, the Y.M.C.A. choir was still singing:

There's no discouragement
Will make him once relent
His first avowed intent
  To be a pilgrim.